Jubilee

Jubilee

PATRICIA REILLY GIFF

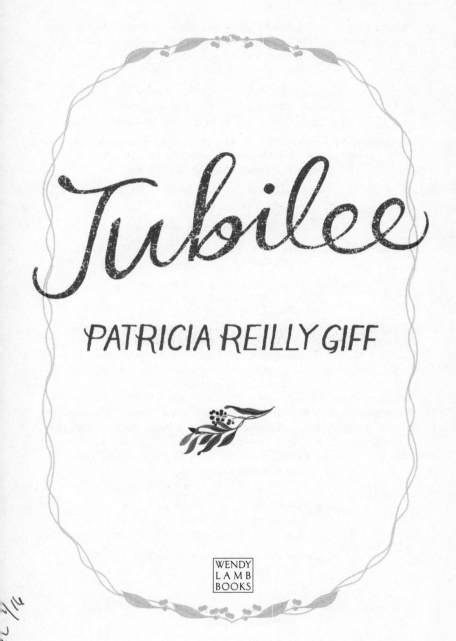

WENDY
LAMB
BOOKS

Text copyright © 2016 by Patricia Reilly Giff
Jacket art copyright © 2016 by Dawn Cooper
Illustrations copyright © 2016 by Sarah Hokanson

Visit us on the Web! randomhousekids.com

Educators and librarians, for a variety of teaching tools, visit us at
RHTeachersLibrarians.com

Library of Congress Cataloging-in-Publication Data
Names: Giff, Patricia Reilly, author.
Title: Jubilee / Patricia Reilly Giff.
Description: First Edition. | New York : Wendy Lamb Books, [2016] |
Summary: "Judith stopped talking long ago when Mom left her in the care
of beloved Aunt Cora. Going back into a regular fifth-grade classroom won't
be easy, but she has her Dog and new friend who will help her through"—
Provided by publisher.
Identifiers: LCCN 2015045694 | ISBN 978-0-385-74486-7 (hardback) |
ISBN 978-0-385-74487-4 (lib. bdg.) | ISBN 978-0-385-74488-1 (ebook)
Subjects: | CYAC: Selective mutism—Fiction. | Dogs—Fiction. | Mothers
and daughters—Fiction. | Friendship—Fiction. | Schools—Fiction. |
Islands—Fiction. | BISAC: JUVENILE FICTION / Family / General
(see also headings under Social Issues).
Classification: LCC PZ7.G3626 Ju 2016 | DDC [Fic]—dc23

The text of this book is set in 13-point Bembo.
The illustrations were rendered in pencil.
Interior design by Trish Parcell

Printed in the United States of America
10 9 8 7 6 5 4 3 2 1
First Edition

Love and welcome to our darling,
Haylee Elizabeth,
born May 8, 2015,
who listened intently
as I read my first book to her
at age five weeks.
And for her mom, Christine Elizabeth,
who has enriched our lives.

Summer's End

CHAPTER 1

*T*he last day of freedom. School tomorrow!

I sat on the edge of the wharf, legs dangling, holding my pad and pencils.

I drew a kid with red hair and green eyes, brows a little thick. I used quick lines for a pointy nose, and a squirrely nest of corkscrews for the hair.

It was turning out to be a girl like me, Judith Ann Magennis.

I tapped the pencil. What was missing?

Of course, the mouth.

My pencil hovered over the blank space. I tore the paper out of the pad, scrunched it up, and tossed it into the water.

Maybe like a mother who'd toss a kid away.

I hid my pad and pencils under a rock and slid down under the wharf to cool off. Water swished in, and I spread my hands like starfish to capture bits of shells.

Noise exploded above me—pounding on the wooden planks.

"I'm going to get you!" a voice yelled.

Me? I ducked under the water and came up dripping. I listened as feet barreled out to the deep end. Not me after all.

"Yeow!" someone yelled, and there was a huge splash.

I peered out from behind a splintery piling. What was going on?

"Serves you right, Mason!" the voice shouted. "Keep your hands off my books. Fingerprints all over them!"

Mason. I knew who he was. He was always a mess. Once I'd seen him rolling down the hill with his brother. He was on the bottom, then winning, on top, grass stains and mud all over him.

I glanced up through the spaces in the wharf and caught a glimpse of his brother, Jerry, who walked away, acting as if he owned the world.

In the water, Mason was a perfect cartoon, mouth open, sputtering, hair plastered to his head.

He swam around the side of the wharf and scrambled up onto the sand. Then he was gone.

I climbed up to the wharf and shook my hair dry. I loved this island. In the distance I could see the coast of Maine, a misty purple blur. And across from me were

4

wooden walls that creaked and groaned when the ferry edged into the slip.

My mother had left on that ferry when I was a toddler, dropping me off at Aunt Cora's as if I were a bundle of laundry.

She sent presents at Christmas and cards on my birthday, postmarked Oakdale, or Vista, or even Apple Valley. She signed them *Mom,* or *Mother,* or her name, *Amber.* She didn't even know what to call herself.

A small boat sped by, sending up a curved wake. A man at the tiller turned off the motor and shouted back at me. "Hey, kid!"

I raised my hand to wave.

"Want a dog?"

Before I could move, he'd picked up a dog and dropped him into the water. "Can't keep him." He switched on the motor again and veered toward open water.

The dog struggled, paddling against the boat's wake.

Poor dog.

Without thinking, I raced along the wharf and dived into the water.

There was a fierce riptide here. It made no difference to me. Gideon, the ferry boat captain, had taught me to swim by the time I was three.

"Swim with the tide, then around it," he'd told me. "Don't fight it."

But the dog was fighting; I could see how tired he was. And soon he'd pass the end of the island and be swept out to sea.

I couldn't speak, but I could certainly swim! I took long, sure strokes and kicked hard and evenly.

When I was close to him, I grabbed the narrow blue collar around his neck, but it came apart in my hand. I gripped a handful of his thick fur; then, with one arm around his neck, I swam back to shore.

CHAPTER 2

*W*e lay there on the warm sand, Dog's great dark eyes on me. When his fur was dried and combed, it would be close to the color of my hair, only lighter. Now he was shivering and cold, but more than that, he was afraid. I rolled in close to him, hugging him to me, warming him.

Did I want a dog? Oh, yes! And I was sure Aunt Cora would be glad to let me have him. I put my mouth against that matted fur and whispered, "You're home, Dog. You'll never have to see the terrible man on the boat again."

He couldn't hear me. There was only one place I could speak loud enough to be heard, and it was all the way up the hill, deep inside Ivy Cottage. But I felt the syrup of happiness being with this dog. He was feeling it too.

Then I remembered. Aunt Cora had sat next to me

at breakfast this morning. In her slow, deliberate way, she'd begun: "You'll be in a new class this year, a regular fifth grader, with thirteen boys and girls."

No more special class? No more Mrs. Leahy and four other kids?

"Why shouldn't you be in a regular class?" Aunt Cora said. "Because you don't speak? You do other things." She counted on her fingers. "You're a great reader. You do math problems faster than I can. Your cartoons are spectacular." She gave me a quick hug. "And most of all, you'll be with more kids. You'll make friends, Jubilee."

That's what she called me: Jubilee. "You're a celebration!" she always said.

Some celebration!

Mrs. Leahy, my old teacher, called me Judy. Gideon, the ferry captain, called me Red because of my Pippi Longstocking hair. And Sophie's five-year-old brother, Travis, called me No-Talk Girl.

Sophie.

Before first grade, Sophie and I were best friends. We dug tiny gardens together. We gathered stones and built houses that toppled into each other and made us laugh.

But one day, I'd heard Jenna ask, "How can you be friends with a weirdo like Judith, who doesn't talk?"

So no more building, no more friend.

I stood now and squeezed water out of my shorts.

Dog stood next to me, shaking himself, drops of water flying.

It was time to look at that fifth-grade classroom. I pulled my pad from under the rock, then started toward Shore Road.

Dog didn't follow. His tail wagged uncertainly.

I went back and ran my hands over his head, down his back. We belonged together. I wanted him to know that.

I walked a few feet, and still he watched. Then, at last, he took a step toward me. A moment later, we loped along the road together.

In back of the school, I raised myself on tiptoe to see inside my new room. Desks were scattered every which way, and the chalkboard was dusty.

A new teacher danced across the front, her sandy hair in ringlets. She glanced toward the window, then went to the chalkboard and wrote her name: *Ms. Quirk.* Underneath she wrote *WELCOME*.

Had she seen me? I raised my hand to wave, but a ball smashed into the windowsill, just missing me. It bounced back against the cement and rolled away across the yard.

I turned. Mason! Why would he try to hit me? No wonder his brother was after him.

I gave Dog a pat, and then we ran past the school and tore up the dirt road toward Windy Hill and Ivy Cottage.

It really wasn't a cottage anymore. The roof had caved in and vines covered the whole thing, so no one else knew it was there. It was almost mine.

Halfway there, Dog paused, nose twitching, tail high. What had he heard?

Was Mason following us? Then I saw what Dog had spotted on the ground: old branches were piled together with a row of stones in front.

Someone's hiding spot.

A very messy one.

A face peered out at me: a mop of pale hair, blue eyes, and more freckles than I could count. It was Sophie's little brother, Travis. He grinned, showing a missing front tooth. With a rustle of leaves, he disappeared again.

Dog sat in front of the hiding spot, whining in a *let's play* voice, until Travis poked his head out again. His finger went to his lips. "Shhh."

I nodded. He'd escaped from Sophie. He did that all the time. I'd hear her calling, her voice loud, then whistling shrilly. Sometimes I'd hear him laughing.

"You can come in, No-Talk Girl," he said. "It's my best place. But it's a secret. Sophie will make me go home and wash my face and say my numbers. She's a bossy girl, and I'm not a baby, you know."

Dog and I crawled inside. Next to Travis was a book with a torn cover, a bag of half-chewed orange slices, and a pencil and paper. "You can draw me while I read," he said.

I smoothed out the paper and drew a cartoon—a boy with a swirl of a hair, laughing eyes, and an upside-down book—while he made up a story about a girl who didn't speak.

Dog's head went up again. Travis put his hand over his mouth.

Mason walked by, his feet crunching on old leaves. If he'd looked down he'd have seen us, but he kept going.

Why had Mason thrown the ball at me? Just mean, maybe. I'd stay away from him.

I signed the cartoon *Judith Magennis,* handed it to Travis, and went with Dog to hang out at Ivy Cottage.

CHAPTER 3

We waded through mounds of weeds, and in front of us, the cottage steps gaped like Travis's missing tooth. I could put my fists through the holes in the walls.

I pushed open the door, feeling the chipped paint under my fingers, and went into the living room.

Dog raised his head, sniffing at this new place. He wasn't a puppy, but he wasn't fully grown either. Where had he been? How could his owner have let him go?

I went toward the bedroom, my hands trailing along the buckling hall walls. The bed was still there, with a flowered spread that had tiny bites along the edge. Maybe the missing pieces were in mice beds deep in the house.

I sank down in front of the old mirror. It had a sil-very look to it, and a crack that ran down one side. I could almost see myself.

"Hey." My voice sounded rusty. Maybe because I could speak only here.

I grinned. "Who's the fairest of them all?" I asked, remembering the evil queen in Snow White.

"Not the fairest, not even close," I answered.

Dog padded into the room and sat close to me.

I leaned my head against the mirror, carefully, so I didn't knock it over. No wonder Sophie thought I was weird. Something had to be crazy about a girl who talked to a mirror instead of people, a girl whose mother took off and left her.

But Mr. Kaufmann, the school psychologist, thought I was fine; so did Aunt Cora. I put my hand on Dog's soft muzzle.

"I love you, Dog," I whispered, surprised that I was able to talk to him. "You don't think I'm weird, right?"

He gave my wrist a quick kiss.

I looked closer into the mirror and began to sing like Gideon did, in a deep voice but with no words. I'd forgotten them. "La, la, tra-la."

Dog squeezed his eyes shut. Maybe he thought I was the worst singer he'd ever heard?

I snapped my mouth shut. Opened it again. "Please," I said to the mirror. "Let me be a regular kid."

Next to me, Dog's flat tongue was out; he was panting. He must be thirsty. I was really thirsty too.

We walked down the hall with its broken tile floor.

Outside, we jogged around the back of the pond. I waited so Dog could drink; then I bent over, holding my hair back with one hand, and slurped in that cool clear water.

Afterward, I sat cartooning while he chased a butter-fly, and then we headed home to see what Aunt Cora would say about him.

School Begins

CHAPTER 4

I woke to hear Aunt Cora calling, "Everything's laid out for you, Jubilee."

I opened my eyes. Next to me, on the bed, Dog stretched. Yesterday afternoon, we'd walked into the kitchen together, and Aunt Cora had knelt on the floor to pat him. "Yes," she said. "I should have known we needed a dog."

I drew the man on the boat for her, and her eyes widened. "Who could do such a thing!" she said, rubbing Dog's ears.

She filled a bowl with leftover meat loaf and we watched while Dog scarfed it up. He was hungry, starving. If only I had known that!

But now, this morning, I looked at the clothes on my dresser: new jeans and a purple shirt with matching hair clips.

I climbed out of bed and knelt on the floor next to

Dog. His tail wagged; he was happy. How could he know this was a sad day for me?

I dressed and grabbed my cartoon pad. *You'll be fine,* I told myself.

That's almost what Aunt Cora said as she put a plate of pancakes with blueberry smiles in front of me. "You'll be amazing, Jubilee." She leaned forward, smelling like the roses in her garden. "It's just today. You'll have the whole weekend before it begins again. A huge scoop of time."

Dog came into the kitchen, and Aunt Cora bent down to pet him. "A perfect dog, a perfect pet," she said. She stood and dropped two more blueberries on my plate. "Two wishes."

I held up two fingers, reached for my pad, and drew a dripping wet boy with a turned-down mouth and nasty eyes. I put an X right down the middle of him.

"A mean boy?" Aunt Cora guessed.

I picked up my spoon and dripped a perfect blob of maple syrup over his head to make her grin.

Aunt Cora was waiting, so I drew in a fat fish with googly eyes. "Ah, fishing," she said. "I wish we could do that today."

She popped a blueberry into her mouth. "My wishes: A new kitchen floor. A motorcycle."

I grinned. I couldn't imagine Aunt Cora riding a motorcycle. Maybe she had secret wishes too. But she went on. "I'd like to be fast instead of slow, instead of thinking things over. I'd race around the island—" She broke off, both of us laughing now.

After breakfast, I tucked my pad in my pocket and searched the closet for a plaid blanket I'd had when I was little. It would be fine for Dog today. I put it in my backpack with a bottle of water and a plastic bowl.

"You'll love your new class," Aunt Cora called after me. "Wait and see."

I wasn't great at waiting. But I pictured Ms. Quirk, and the yellow *WELCOME* on the board. Maybe it would work out.

From the window, I saw Mason trudging toward the top of the island, away from school. Toward Ivy Cottage? I bit my lip. There was nothing I could do about it.

Back in the hall Aunt Cora smoothed down my hair and held out a lunch bag with a salami sandwich, my favorite. "And a peach to keep you sweet!"

I reached up and kissed her soft cheek.

She hesitated. "I could walk you halfway."

I shook my head. I was all right. I took the back way past Sophie's house to reach the maple tree on the side of the school.

I spread the small blanket under the lowest branch of the tree. Dog was amazing. He knew just what to do. He circled around until his tail met his nose and closed his eyes. I left a bowl of water beside him.

Maybe I'd see him from the classroom. It was the best I could do.

Inside, kids slammed doors and ran down the hall; some of them went into Room Fourteen. But I walked toward the classroom like a snail and went inside.

"I'm happy to see you," Ms. Quirk said, and I nodded, going to stand against the side wall.

Where was Sophie?

"Glad you're here too," the teacher told Harry.

"Yeah." He looked as if he wanted to be anywhere else.

Ms. Quirk had written our names out on cards, one on each desk. "Look for yours. That will be your space."

I found my name on a desk near the window. I could even see Dog under the maple tree.

Mason came in at last, out of breath. He had the face of the bait-selling man on the wharf who was mean and miserable and didn't mind selling those poor little killies that were headed for a nasty end in the mouths of some large fish.

He slid into the seat next to me, his shirt filled with crumbs. He kicked against the rungs of his desk. On the front of one sneaker was an inked-in *JW,* his brother Jerry's initials.

He was skinny as a spider, with knobby knees. But I didn't bother to take another look at his bait-man face, or his crumb-y shirt.

Ms. Quirk perched herself on the edge of a table, her arms out as if she wanted to hug all of us. "This is my first year of teaching, and the first year on an island. We'll make it a year of firsts." Clink went the bangles on her wrists.

If I could have a year of firsts, I'd see my mother. Sophie and I would be friends again. I'd speak!

Every time I saw him, Mr. Kaufmann always said, "Everything is right around the corner, Judith. You just have to make it happen."

But how?

CHAPTER 5

*T*he sky was sunny blue, a great no-school day. But Ms. Quirk wasn't thinking about the sky. "Pull up your chairs," she said. "We'll get to know each other."

Kids dragged their chairs to the front, almost like a cattle stampede.

Harry and Conor weren't interested in getting to know each other. They played pencil hockey at their desks. "Peshuum!" Conor yelled and erasers blasted across the room.

One almost hit Mason, who was staring out the window.

What would he do?

But he just grinned at them.

That was strange for a boy who'd thrown a ball trying to take off my head!

It was even noisier in the classroom now. Up front,

Maddie was telling her life story. Everyone else was whispering. It was a boring life story.

If I went out the open door, no one would even notice I was gone. I'd take a quick walk down the hall, run outside to see if Dog was all right, and be back by the time Maddie had gotten up to her life in kindergarten.

I tiptoed around the side of the room, staring at the thick white tiles underneath my feet. In the hall, everything was quiet, almost like the empty school in the summertime.

Halfway down was a big window. Usually it was dusty with dried-up raindrops. But Ciro, the custodian, had washed it so it sparkled. I had to stay away from him. If he saw me, he'd send me straight back to Room Fourteen, talking about how important learning was.

I leaned closer to the window and saw Dog sleeping. Then I spotted Sophie walking Travis across the yard. He was crying, rubbing his eyes. "I don't want to go to school!" His legs churned, kicking everything in his way.

And Sophie was in his way. "That hurt, Travis." She bent to rub her knee.

"Travis is not easy to handle," Aunt Cora's friend Mary said the other day. "Especially when his poor mother works nights as a nurse in a hospital on the mainland. She needs a couple of hours of sleep during the day to keep herself going, for pity's sake."

I remembered crying at night for my mother. Aunt Cora had sat at the side of the bed, weighing it down a little, humming, holding my hands with her large warm ones.

Travis needed an Aunt Cora.

The hall wasn't empty anymore. Sophie had gotten Travis as far as the kindergarten door. He was holding on to the molding, shaking his head.

"You have to go in, Travis." She sounded desperate. "You're making us both late."

If I could go over to him, I'd put my hands on his shoulders. I'd rock him back and forth until he was peaceful. I knew what was wrong. Travis wanted to be a big boy, but school was too much for him. I remembered that: the huge school, all those new faces. And everyone seemed to know what they were doing, except me.

I went forward. Travis turned to me, but Sophie pulled him behind her. I had a quick memory of Jenna asking her, *How can you be friends with a weirdo?*

I stepped away, my hands up to let her know that I'd just wanted to help.

"Nobody wants you," she said in a voice so low I barely heard. But tears flooded my eyes. I backed down the hall and put my hand on the outside door.

Windy Hill, I told myself. I'd look down at the shimmering sea with the white foam breakers, and watch the egret and herons that swooped over the pond.

I pushed open the door. Outside, I swiped at my eyes and ran across the schoolyard, stopping to run my hand over Dog's head.

He jumped up to follow me. We went through the gate and up the dirt road.

No one had seen me. No one knew I was gone yet. I'd sit on the steps at Ivy Cottage and draw. I'd try not to think about what Sophie had said. *Nobody wants you.*

CHAPTER 6

$\mathscr{I}$ caught my breath as we reached the pond in back of Ivy Cottage. My friend, Mr. Kaufmann, had said once, "We're not fast enough to run away from sorrow."

I knew he was right; he was always right. But that's just what I'd tried to do now.

The sun blasted into my eyes. I wiggled out of my jeans, unclipped my hair, and slid into the pond. Dog stood on the edge. I held out my arm, so he'd know it was safe, but he sank down, watching.

I put my face in the water and swam across with slow strokes. I tried to pretend it was still summer, and the school was locked up tight.

Think about cool water. About Aunt Cora and Gideon. And Dog with his velvet ears.

It was Friday. No school until Monday, and Gideon would take me out in his boat tomorrow night; he'd sing in a booming voice, telling me that he wanted the fish to hear.

I floated, thinking about my mother. I didn't know what she looked like, even though I'd seen pictures. Her head was turned in one; her hand was up in another; a third was blurred. I'd made dozens of cartoon faces trying to guess. Long hair? Red like mine? Tall or tiny? Skinny or plump like Aunt Cora? I gave her words: *I've missed you, Judith. My leaving was a mistake. I'm coming back.*

If only I could send a message: *I'll never do one thing wrong if only you'd come home.*

I swam back toward Dog, came out of the water shivering, and dressed quickly. As we walked around to the front of the house, I listened to crickets rubbing their legs together in a rusty song. A V of geese flew high overhead, honking.

Everything made a noise; everything talked.

We walked around to the front of the house. I stopped. Something felt different. Hadn't I closed the door when I left last time?

I knew I had. I wanted to be sure the possums and raccoons left the house to the mice and chipmunks with their dozens of secret entrances.

Had someone been here?

I tiptoed into the living room; silky sand drifted up in the corners. It was just as I left it. The kitchen with its unpainted wooden walls was fine too: the

stove door wide open so mice wouldn't trap themselves inside.

Something was different in the hall, though. The
print of a shoe tip, or a sneaker, was marked on the
sandy floor.

Just the tip.

Someone really had been here.

I leaned against the bedroom door, looking in at
the almost empty room with its silver mirror. Who
might it have been?

There wasn't time to figure it out. A horn blasted.
Gideon had nosed the ferry into the boat slip. St. Pas-
cal's Church bells chimed.

Nearly the whole day had gone.

Closing the door firmly behind us, I glanced around
for a decent-sized rock.

I found one on the side path: easy to roll, but big
enough to be noticed.

It was a fine message—*Keep out, whoever you are. You
don't belong here.*

I edged it up against the front door, pulled a tangle
of vines over it, and headed home with Dog. We'd
be there ahead of Aunt Cora, who took care of the
church, putting yellow and white chrysanthemums in
the altar vases.

But who was sitting on the stone wall right outside
our house? I stopped short, almost stepping on Dog's
thumping tail.

Ms. Quirk! She saw me and unfolded herself from the wall, stretching a little.

Dog knew this was unusual. He circled around me, resting his large back paws on my feet.

"I had a dog like yours when I was eleven years old," Ms. Quirk said. "Her name was Princess."

Why was she talking about dogs? She really must have wondered where I'd been all day.

Dog sat up higher on my toes.

The church bells chimed once: four-thirty.

"I missed you, Judith," Ms. Quirk said. "I didn't like to see your empty chair all day."

I could hardly look at her.

She spoke softly. "I came from clear across the country to teach here."

I tilted my head. Like my mother, in California.

"I want to help you, Judith." She hesitated. "But if you leave school, we'll both be in trouble. The principal came in today and saw that you were gone."

Mrs. Ames. Trouble.

"This could be a wonderful year," she said. "There are so many things for us to do. Outdoor things, indoor things."

She held out two pieces of yellow paper. "One is a permission slip, the other is homework."

I went toward her slowly, taking the papers. But she wasn't finished.

"Everyone has a secret world," she said.

Ivy Cottage and the silver mirror!

"So many creatures live here on the island." She held up her hand. "Deer and coyotes." She waved her hands. "Birds. Fish."

She smiled. "We'll uncover things about them, where they live, what they have for supper maybe." She tilted her head. "We can't appreciate things"—she hesitated again—"or people . . . unless we know them."

Did she mean me?

But she went on. "We'll have partners to do it."

She touched my shoulder. "So I'll see you Monday?"

I nodded.

"All day." She went down the road, waving over her shoulder.

Inside, I looked through the cabinets for a snack.

Uncovering wildlife?

With partners?

I opened the refrigerator and felt the rush of cold air. I leaned in, my head against an icy bottle of milk.

Friday! The whole weekend ahead.

WISHING

CHAPTER 7

$\mathcal{I}$ sipped from a glass of icy milk and Dog slurped down about a gallon of water from his new bowl in the corner. He was getting to know this kitchen, our house. I hoped he knew that I loved him, that he'd be here forever.

I put my glass in the sink and went along the back hall to my bedroom. There were things to figure out before Aunt Cora came home from decorating the altar at church.

I sat on my bed with the quilt Aunt Cora had patched together for me. It was a sea of blues and greens, like the water that surrounded our island on a peaceful day. Eyes burning, I looked at the curtains that blew against the screen, and the blue-violet rag rug that Aunt Cora and I had made together.

Mrs. Ames would call to say I'd left school, I was sure of it.

How could I explain to Aunt Cora what had happened? I'd never want her to know what Sophie had said, those terrible words: *Nobody wants you.*

Dog stood at the bottom of the bed until I patted the quilt. Then he jumped up with me, and I rubbed his ears.

The phone began to ring.

Mrs. Ames?

The screen door opened. Aunt Cora was home from church.

Dog looked toward the bedroom door, and then at me. Maybe he knew trouble was on its way.

I slid off the bed and walked down the hall.

Aunt Cora stood there, her purse slung over one arm, smiling at me, and before she could reach for it, the phone stopped ringing.

Maybe Mrs. Ames would forget by Monday.

Get real, Judith.

Aunt Cora saw my face. "Something's wrong? Something in school?"

My eyes slid away from hers.

The phone began to ring again.

She dropped her purse on the hall table and picked up the phone. "Hello." She made circles on the rug with one plump foot. "Um-hum," she said. "Oh, yes. Oh, um-hum."

Mrs. Ames's voice was angry; it was loud. I could almost hear what she was saying.

I sat on the stairs leading to the attic and leaned my

head against the railing, the slats hard against my fore-head. Then the phone call was over.

Aunt Cora sat on the step just below me. "I was the one. I was determined that you belonged in a regular class. I told Mrs. Ames that you didn't have to speak to get along. I went up there and demanded . . ."

Demanded. I rolled that word around in my head, staring down at her soft curls on the step below me. I couldn't imagine Aunt Cora demanding anything.

"I want everything for you." Her voice was thick. "If they only knew you the way I do."

Dog stood in the hall, just below Aunt Cora, and put his head on her lap.

He couldn't imagine why she was crying, but he knew something was wrong.

"The day you came . . . ," Aunt Cora began.

The day my mother left.

"I was right here in the hall. The front door opened and you stood there, your mother behind you, her suit-case in her hand. She was on the way across the coun-try, ready to be an actress or a writer. She was so young to be a mother. Too young."

Across the country, almost like Ms. Quirk.

Aunt Cora cleared her throat. "You stood at the window, looking after her, such a little girl. I could see your reflection in the glass, your woebegone face. I knew it was going to be hard for you, but I didn't know how hard."

I was sure she was going to say I'd stopped speaking then. But she put her hand on my shoulder. "For me, it was a miracle! A child to love. A jubilee."

She sighed. "Later I started you in a little Sunday church group. You were the only one without a mother, and I think you wondered what the other children thought. You still said a few words. But then . . ." She raised her shoulders. "You stopped talking."

I began to cry without a sound, warm tears sliding down my cheeks. I wasn't crying like Travis whose mouth opened wide; his screaming was so loud I could hear it from wherever I was. It would have been a relief to cry that way.

"I've never loved anyone the way I've loved you, Jubilee," Aunt Cora said.

I bent forward and put my arms around her neck. Warm. Safe.

She reached up and put her hand over one of mine. "It's going to be all right someday, Jubilee. You'll talk when the time is right."

That was what Mr. Kaufmann had said.

"But in the meantime . . ."

I knew what was coming.

"Mrs. Ames will give you only one more chance. Otherwise you'll be back in the special class."

I patted her shoulder and nodded. I couldn't remember that day at the window. Or could I? My mother on the path, looking back at me, raising her hand to wave.

And Aunt Cora! How lucky I was to have her. She wasn't my mother. So I couldn't love her the way I loved my mother with her question mark face.

But still . . .

We stood up, all three of us. "Let's have a garden and cheese dinner." Aunt Cora wiped her eyes and ran her hand over Dog's broad back.

Outside, we walked around her garden and tore off lettuce leaves; we dropped plum tomatoes into a strainer, and shredded bits of basil on top.

I had one more chance. No matter what Sophie said, no matter what anyone said, I was going to stay in that classroom. I was beginning to like Ms. Quirk, who'd had a dog named Princess. I wanted to know about the wildlife on the island. What had she said? Something like *You can't appreciate creatures unless you know them.*

And I wanted to get to know them. And maybe I wanted a partner too.

CHAPTER 8

$\mathcal{I}$ slid dishes and glasses onto the table for Saturday-night dinner as Gideon burst in the front door, his boots loud on the hall floor. "I hope it's not liver. I hope it's not pork chops," he sang.

At the table, Aunt Cora and I glanced at each other. Gideon always made us laugh. He filled the kitchen with his huge self, his great grin.

Dog backed under the table. He rested his head on his paws, unsure about Gideon. But Gideon reached into his pocket. "Cora told me about you this morning." His voice was softer than usual. He held out a dog biscuit.

Dog hesitated, then moved forward, tail thumping on the floor as he took the biscuit. He stretched out under the table while we ate scallops in a thick white sauce. Aunt Cora and Gideon loved scallops.

Actually, they were almost as bad as liver or pork

chops. Even Dog just sniffed at the one I sneaked to him.

We ate quickly because Gideon and I were going out in his small motorboat, to putter around the island. We'd watch the sun roll down below the horizon, and maybe I'd draw cartoon gulls with baseball hats, or fish with eyeglasses popping up to have a look at the horizon.

Most of the time I'd take the tiller, guiding us wherever I wanted to go.

Best of all, Gideon and I were quiet. He didn't mind my not speaking. Not one bit.

"Back soon," he told Aunt Cora on our way out the door. "Unless Red and I decide to head for the Fiji Islands."

I put my hand out, in a *stay there* motion, and Dog closed his eyes.

Halfway to the wharf, Gideon stopped. "Someone is coming with us tonight, Red. A new partner on our Saturday night ocean voyage."

I walked around him and went toward the boat. Saturday nights were Gideon's and mine, not a new partner's.

Gideon followed. "A nice kid. Big family."

A girl with a big family?

The island wasn't that big. Maybe someone had just moved across from the mainland.

But suppose she wanted to take the tiller?

To decide where we'd go?

To talk when Gideon and I were quiet?

I closed my eyes and shut out those thoughts. I was looking for a friend, wasn't I?

"A good worker too," Gideon went on. "Scrubbed the deck the other day. Wait till you see it."

Scrubbing out the boat. Smelly. Sticky. Gideon and I hated to do it.

I looked up at Gideon's face. How old was she?

Gideon read my mind. "The same age as you, Red. And you need a better friend than an old guy like me."

I ducked my head to show him I wasn't Saturday-night happy, but he didn't notice. He wasn't always as good with my signals as Aunt Cora was.

We stepped onto the wharf; I breathed in the smell of the sea and heard the waves lapping against the pilings. In front of us was Gideon's shiny boat, the *Take It Easy*.

Mason sat on the side bench, waiting for us.

Mason!

His leg was bent, and he scratched a mosquito-bitten ankle. He looked like the lone egret that fished at the Ivy Cottage pond.

I climbed onto the boat, angling past his skinny legs, his knobby knees, and his big feet.

I sat as far away from him as I could. It wasn't very far. Gideon's boat wasn't that big.

Gideon jumped in, heavy enough to tilt us sideways, a feeling I usually loved.

"Mason," he said. "This is Judith."

"Hi," Mason said to my back.

Gideon revved up the motor. "Want to take her out, Red?"

At least he hadn't asked Mason.

I wanted to show Mason I could do that easily. But I'd have to scramble past him again.

I shook my head and looked straight ahead at the small boats docked on our starboard side. As we passed, each one rocked from our wake.

We motored out on that calm water, Gideon singing in his deep voice. I drew gulls getting ready for the night, one wearing a pair of striped pajamas, the other with a puffy nightcap.

I turned, just an inch, so I could see what Mason was doing. His head was tilted as he watched a pair of large gray gulls circle, then dive into the water for their dinner.

Under my feet, the deck was clean. Gideon was right. Mason had done a good job, which made me feel worse.

Maybe Mason would be around forever: in my classroom, on our boat.

Maybe even at Ivy Cottage.

I swallowed, then began a wishing game that Aunt Cora and I played at breakfast. Sometimes they're silly wishes, like sailing to Antarctica after lunch. But sometimes serious ones, like my mother coming in on the ferry.

"Judith," she'd call. "Get your pad, your favorite straw hat, and climb aboard. We're leaving this minute. Wave goodbye to Mason."

A motorboat chugged past us now, throwing up waves that splashed over the side of our boat.

Mason jumped.

Without thinking, I looked straight into his eyes. I didn't care if he could see I was angry.

Hadn't he invaded the seat next to me in my new classroom?

And now he'd taken my favorite seat on this boat.

What nerve!

Gideon veered around the side of the island, going west, straight into the sun.

I squinted at the glowing path the sun sent across the sea. I could almost reach out and run my fingers through the liquid gold water.

If only my mother could see that water and hear Gideon's warm voice singing "Red Sails in the Sunset."

Maybe she'd want to come back home to our island.

CHAPTER 9

*C*uddled under my quilt on Sunday morning, there was just enough time to draw a cartoon of Dog. He lay on his back, tongue lolling, all four paws in the air.

"Ah, no school today, I'm free as a bird," said the bubble over his head. Me too!

Aunt Cora and I walked to church. On the way, we heard the organ playing and Gideon singing "Bread of Angels." Inside, there were chrysanthemums in silver vases and green bows on the altar.

I prayed, *Let me open my mouth. Let me sing.* I opened my mouth, but nothing came out.

That was what happened every Sunday.

But after church, I remembered: homework!

It was a day filled with sunshine, a sky that was totally blue; leaves fluttered in the breeze. But I went to my room to find the yellow homework paper that rested under my bed with a few dust balls.

Choose one living thing from the island. Can you tell something about it? We want to know.

Actually not such a bad assignment. I might sit under the wharf and find a sea star, or maybe a killy that'd escaped from the bait man's trap.

But suppose Mason was there?

I leaned forward. "We've had enough of Mason, right?" I whispered to sleeping Dog.

He opened one eye.

I tucked the paper into one pocket and my cartoon book into the other and went down the hall with Dog behind me, yawning.

Aunt Cora pattered back and forth in the kitchen. She was beginning to fix dinner for later: ham and beans thick with molasses, and a spinach salad with apple slices from the tree in the garden. It would be hours before we ate.

"Love you, Jubilee," Aunt Cora said as I headed for the door.

I grinned at her and tapped the molding. Sometimes the tap meant *I love you too.* Sometimes it meant *I'm on my way out.* And sometimes it didn't mean anything more than *It's a great day.* Aunt Cora could always figure it out.

Outside, the day was warm, but I could feel fall in the air. As I walked, a single orange leaf fluttered from a maple tree, and two perfect red leaves lay on the path. I reached down and tucked one inside my pad.

Summer was almost over.

I stopped in front of Ivy Cottage, remembering the shoe print I'd seen on the sandy floor.

I moved the rock and took the old broom from the ruined steps. Someone had rested it against the wooden railing a long time ago, and most of the straw must have become part of some bird's nest.

I took it inside, and tried not to look at the print. But my eyes went toward that mark . . .

It was gone.

The grains of sand had rearranged themselves. Maybe a cool wind had come in through the broken window and changed the pattern.

I swept anyway.

Down the hall.

In the corners . . .

And glanced in the living room.

Another print.

I stood still, listening.

The caw of a crow sounded outside. Inside, it was silent except for the swish of the broom and my sneakers as I swept over the print in the living room. A drift of sand remained in the doorway.

But that was all right.

Sand belonged.

"Let's go to the pond," I whispered to Dog, and we headed outside, sinking down beside each other in the oozy grass on the edge.

An egret swooped in on the other side. It was fierce-looking, with its crested head and eyes like shiny blue jewels. Eyes that saw all those poor fish under the surface. They'd never have a chance against that egret.

Egret was not going to be on my yellow paper!

Gideon said everyone had to eat. True. But the egret was very sneaky about it.

I leaned forward, my fingers dabbling in the cool water. Maybe I'd known all weekend what I wanted to write about.

Two years ago, during a storm, a branch had fallen into the pond. Pieces of the wood had decayed so one end of it looked like lace. And now, in the center, a bale of turtles sunned themselves.

As soon as they saw my shadow, they slid into the water and disappeared.

I wrote about them: their shiny dark shells, their terrific night vision. I said that turtles had been around for more than a hundred million years, and the best part, some of them liked to play.

I knew about them from a library book I read last year. I thought more about what Ms. Quirk had said. If you knew about something, maybe you appreciate it.

I certainly liked turtles. Was it because I understood them?

Once Gideon said that a snapping turtle had eyes close to the top of its head. At the bottom of the pond it could look up and watch the rest of the world go by.

I poked my toes into the water. It was colder than it had been all summer. Turtles were cold-blooded, their temperature the same as the water. I tried to pretend I didn't mind the cold either.

I'm brave, I told myself, and Dog tilted his head, watching me.

I tucked the turtle paper under a rock. I hoped Ms. Quirk wouldn't mind the splotches of water from my wet fingers.

Then I dashed into the pond, clothes and all. I dived underneath, and came up sputtering.

It was freezing!

I began to swim, taking long strokes until I was warm. Then I floated on my back, watching the clouds make patterns in the sky.

Dog barked and I raised my head, but he'd turned away from me, staring at the trees and the dirt path that led away from the pond.

Was someone there?

I dived, swimming fast underwater, and in moments I was out of the pond.

Dog had stopped barking; he wasn't even looking toward the trees anymore.

I was shivering. I wiped my hands on my jeans, picked up the yellow paper with two fingers, and started down the path.

Halfway down, I saw what Dog had seen.

Travis was curled up underneath a sycamore tree, turning the pages of a picture book.

He'd escaped from Sophie again.

I went quietly, so I wouldn't bother him. Maybe he needed a little time alone, like the turtle. Besides, Sophie didn't want me near him.

Back home, with the sweet smell of molasses wafting through the house, I sat on the back porch, the sun drying my damp clothes.

CHAPTER 10

*A*fter dinner that night, Gideon scraped back his chair.

"You're the world's best cook," he told Aunt Cora on his way out. "And you're the best artist, Red." He tapped the cartoon I'd drawn of her, with a huge flowered apron tied around her waist. Then he went off to captain the ferry to the mainland.

Aunt Cora and I slid bowls into the refrigerator, stacked the plates and put them in the dishwasher.

I swiped the cloth over the table in huge, satisfying swirls and Aunt Cora whistled while she swept the floor. She sounded happy, almost as if she might be a rare bird that had appeared in our kitchen.

When I was in my bedroom, I peered into the mirror and whistled too. . . .

Whistled quietly, but Dog would be able to hear me now.

"It's almost dark," Aunt Cora said in her soft voice. "Let's take a walk and watch the stars come out over the water."

I pulled our sweaters off the hook in the back hall, and draped her sweater over her shoulders. I wrapped mine around my waist, and snapped my fingers so Dog would know I wanted him to come too.

Outside, the katydids' song was loud as they rubbed their forewings together from the treetops. "They're telling us fall is coming," Aunt Cora said.

We passed the wharf and trudged through the sand in our bare feet, cold now without the daytime sun to warm it. "Look up, Jubilee," Aunt Cora said. "There's a sliver of moon, making friends with one bright planet called Venus."

I smiled thinking about it. I loved the way she talked; I always knew what she was thinking. If only I could tell her that.

I looked out at the shimmering water, the gentle waves brushing the shore, and the boats tied up against the wharf.

I saw something else. Dog saw it too.

Someone was hiding in one of those boats, a neat little one with a furled red sail and a name painted on the stern in large black and gray letters: *Escape from the Shore.*

That boat belonged to a friend of Gideon's, another

ferry captain. A friend who was much bigger than the person crouching in the stern!

I kept watching, my hand on Dog's head so he wouldn't bark.

Who could it be?

Ah! It was Mason, hiding in a boat that didn't belong to him.

Was he going to steal it?

Dog gave the tiniest warning, a short gruff sound under his breath.

Someone was running fast along the sand in back of us.

I spun around and Aunt Cora turned.

A barefoot teenager, wearing cutoff jeans, stopped. "I'm looking for my brother, Mason. That kid is such a mess." He bent over, hands on his knees, to catch his breath. "I told him he could borrow my best sneakers, and now they're green. Covered with seaweed. Wait till I get him."

My finger was ready to point. But when I glanced at the boat, I couldn't see Mason. All I saw was the boat rocking gently.

Aunt Cora and the boy looked toward the line of boats. But my eyes were better than theirs. I saw Mason's hands curled around the side of the boat. He was in the water, head submerged.

How long could he hold his breath?

I curled my own fingers against my sides.

Aunt Cora shook her head. "I haven't seen anyone. Just the two of us looking at stars."

The water would be much colder than the sun-warmed pond. I was glad when I saw his head pop up to the surface.

CHAPTER 11

*O*n Monday morning, I was out of bed in a flash, starving. Downstairs, I put kibble into Dog's bowl. Aunt Cora poured orange juice into glasses and spooned raspberries on top of my cereal.

"Make a wish, Jubilee."

I pictured staying home from school forever, wandering around Ivy Cottage and the pond, as Dog and I grew old as redwood trees.

Instead I drew a cartoon of a girl and a dog slurping a dripping ice cream cone. "Yum!" said the balloon over their heads.

"Too early for me," Aunt Cora said, and we grinned at each other.

I remembered the permission slip then and ran to get it. "Lovely field trip." She signed her name. She dropped a kiss on my head and was off to work at the church.

I had at least ten minutes before school, a good feeling. I walked out back and helped myself to a plum from a low-hanging branch. Then I walked slowly along the road with Dog.

Sophie was coming out of her house with Travis. I remembered the stone houses we used to build, and felt that pain in my chest. *Nobody wants you.*

She saw me and would have kept going, but Travis pulled hard on her hand. "There's my friend, the No-Talk Girl."

"Shhh." Sophie gave him a gentle push. "She doesn't talk to us; we don't talk to her." They walked in front of me, Travis waving over his shoulder.

I made fists, my nails digging into my palms, dropping my papers and Dog's blanket. I picked them up slowly, telling myself I didn't care.

Didn't care!

At the maple tree, I flapped the blanket in the air, then let it settle. Dog settled too.

I headed for the school door and turned to look at Dog, but someone was bending over the blanket.

Mason!

I went back to them, almost running. But Mason had disappeared into the trees.

A thick biscuit lay on the edge of the blanket. Dog scarfed it up in two seconds, his tail waving wildly from right to left. That meant he was happy.

Why had Mason done that?

I hated to leave Dog with Mason still outside some-where, but the bell would ring soon.

Inside, teachers walked along the hall, calling hello to each other.

My classroom door was still closed, so I backed up, trying to decide whether to go outside again. But Ms. Quirk padded along in sneakers. A canvas bag was slung over her shoulder, and her arms were loaded with books and small notepapers: blues and pinks, plaids and purples.

The folded notes slid onto the floor that was shiny as an ice skating rink, the notes like small birds. "Help," she said when she saw me.

We scrambled for them, bumping heads. "Sorry." She smiled. "All my partner papers."

She threw open the door, and kids piled in behind us.

"It's too beautiful to be stuck in Room Fourteen all day." She held up her hand. "Drop your permis-sion slips on my desk, and don't forget your homework. And then you'll each get a note with the name of your partner."

I put my turtle paper and the signed permission slip on the corner of her desk and saw my partner note. I opened it.

Sophie!

My mouth went dry.

I spun around; she was right behind me. I watched as she picked up her paper. It had to have my name!

She shook her head, her lips tight.

I went back to my seat, holding my head up. From the corner of my eye, I saw Mason come in.

He slid into his seat. "Thanks."

What did he mean?

"For not telling that I was in the boat."

I raised one shoulder just a bit.

All the notes were taken now. Everyone had a partner. Ms. Quirk clapped her hands. "You're going to work together for the first time today. But now let's get out of here."

Chairs were scraped back. Harry and Conor raced to the door.

"Do you want the whole school to hear?" Ms. Quirk asked, finger on her lips.

We stood still as statues.

"We're going to the field near the water," she said. "Take pencils and paper. We're out to find life." She grinned. "Wild or otherwise."

She gave out cardboard boxes. "We'll collect treasures at the dunes. Shells that once housed creatures. We'll wave *safe trip* to the red-winged blackbirds that are ready to fly south. Sad for them to leave this beautiful island."

She tapped her pencil on a pile of extra paper with a click-click sound, and asked Harry to help her carry the canvas bag to the beach. "Snacks, in case we're hungry."

We marched down the hall, circling Mrs. Ames, and sped out the door, everyone excited: a school day poor Mrs. Leahy would never have imagined.

Outside, it was windy. Leaves and grit blew across the schoolyard; my hair blew too.

"Whew," Ms. Quirk said. "Fall is coming."

I hugged my sweater around me as we walked down the path that led to the dunes.

"Freedom!" Harry yelled.

Conor was yelling too.

I took deep breaths, smelling the damp sand and the sharp scent of the sea.

Dog trotted toward me. He knew he couldn't break into the line, so he fell in behind us, and I edged farther back so we could be together.

Sophie was in the middle of the line, walking fast, as if she wanted to catch up to Ms. Quirk. Mason's seaweed sneakers were moving toward the back. A moment later he was next to me, his hand resting on Dog's head.

Dog gave him a smiling look: his mouth open, his tail high and waving.

I tried not to mind.

"What's his name?" Mason asked.

I pretended I didn't hear.

It was almost as if Mason were talking to himself. "Rebel is a good name for a dog. So is John."

John? I had to smile.

"But this dog?" Mason went on. "This is a terrific dog. I'd call him Faithful."

Faithful was exactly right. I couldn't help myself. I turned to take a quick look at Mason. Not a bait man's face. It was a regular face with freckles dotting his nose; his eyes were green-gray. His scribble-scrabble shirt had a ripped sleeve. But his nails were clean, probably from being in the water last night.

Ms. Quirk stood at the edge of the sand. The reeds brushed against each other with a crackling sound.

She slipped off her sneakers. "You can take off yours too. But walk around the reeds. We don't want to disturb them." She tilted her head. "Besides, they're sharp, and so are the shells."

We left our sneakers in a jumbled pile, while Mason kept talking. "I never had a dog," he said as Ms. Quirk called, "Spread out. Stay with your partners. What can you find here?"

She raised the silver whistle that hung around her neck. "I'll let you know when it's time to eat."

I looked for Sophie, but she was standing next to Ms. Quirk, trying to get her attention. How was she going to tell the teacher that she didn't want to be my partner?

I backed away then, and Dog and I wandered around the reeds, careful not to bend them.

I heard Ms. Quirk tell Conor about a shell she always looked for. "It's called a junonia. It loops around itself with brown square markings. Maybe someday I'll find one."

My bare toe touched something. I bent over to see a messy ball of twigs with a piece of yellow candy wrapper and a few soft feathers threaded inside.

I picked up the nest carefully. One spotted blue egg lay in the center, cracked and empty.

The mother bird and her baby were long gone. I hoped they were together. Gideon told me once that daughter crows came back to their mothers' nests long after they were grown. But this wasn't a crow's nest.

I edged the nest into my cardboard box, but before I could put on the cover, Mason touched my shoulder. "Look at that."

I jumped.

The nest fell out of the box, and the wind picked it up. It flew, end over end, and disappeared into the tall reeds.

I ran toward it, the sand and sharp shells slowing down my feet, Dog crashing along next to me. But it was gone.

"It's my fault," Mason told Ms. Quirk. "I ruined her nest. It even had an empty egg. I never do anything right."

We walked back, passing Sophie, who was bent

over, looking at something with Jenna. Conor was picking up a shell, and Ashton called, "Maybe I found a turtle's egg."

But then, I'd found a nest with an eggshell; I'd run my fingers over the spiky twigs, the cracked shell. Maybe that was enough.

"There's an encyclopedia of birds in the classroom," Ms. Quirk told me. "You'll be able to find out what kind of a bird it was."

But I knew from the blue of its egg it was a robin's nest. It must have blown far, because I didn't think robins nested in the low dunes.

Mason made a sound in his throat. A sad one.

It was a sound I might have made sometimes, if only I could have spoken.

I did something that really surprised me. I took a step toward Mason, who'd never had a dog, who believed he never did anything right.

I went close enough so he'd know I wasn't angry about the nest. And I realized something: Mason would never have tried to hit anyone with a ball. His aim was probably terrible.

Ms. Quirk blew her silver whistle and we gathered around her. She gave out chicken sandwiches she'd made herself, and bottles of cool water.

We sank down in the sand, and she made sure there was a sandwich and water even for Dog.

TOGETHER

CHAPTER 12

On Wednesday, Ms. Quirk said, "I have the best news. Mrs. Ames loves the idea of studying wildlife. She'd be happy if we had an assembly later this fall, to let everyone know what we've been up to. We'll talk about it soon."

An assembly! In front of everyone! That was very scary.

I looked out the window at Dog snoozing on his blanket and smiled. But then I glanced across the classroom at Sophie's empty desk. Of course she didn't want to be my partner.

Ms. Quirk tapped a packet of papers on her desk and grinned at us. "I learned a lot from your weekend homework; the secret lives of animals, birds, and even"—she held up a yellow paper—"a turtle."

She began to read. It was my paper!

I looked out the window, my hands trembling a little. Mrs. Leahy never read our compositions aloud.

Maybe no one was paying attention. But then everyone was laughing, even Ms. Quirk.

I couldn't help looking up. It was a good laugh. She was showing everyone my turtle cartoon.

The door opened and Sophie came in, her face red, her hair escaping from a braid. She sat at her desk, and I watched her from the corner of my eye. She twisted her ankles one way and the other.

Was she worried about Travis?

I thought of his calling me No-Talk Girl. All his talking. His earnest face. His missing tooth. How he wanted to be my friend.

If Travis were my brother, I wouldn't be sitting here twisting my ankles.

Ms. Quirk looked serious. "I've been thinking. I'm going to change some of the partners." She waved my paper. "I think this turtle person should work with another turtle person. And two others wanted to work on squirrels."

Sophie sat up and smiled.

Ms. Quirk turned to her desk to read another change or two.

I stood up quietly, circled the room, and opened the door, holding the knob tightly so a burst of wind wouldn't give me away.

I glanced back to see Mason mouthing something at me.

I hesitated.

"Trouble," he ended.

I figured out the rest: *You're going to get in trouble.*

I peered into the hall. It wouldn't be good if Mrs. Ames was blowing down the hall like the wind. I did see her legs, like large scissors, but they were going the opposite way.

Still, I'd have to walk in her direction to get to Travis's kindergarten.

Instead, halfway down the hall, I went out the door, into the schoolyard. Dog looked up from under the maple tree, but I motioned him to stay, and took a few deep breaths of the late-summer air.

The fourth grade was having early recess, playing volleyball. One of the balls bounced near me. "Hey, kid, get that!" someone yelled, so I kicked it to him.

I ducked under Mrs. Leahy's window and hurried around the side of the building.

Mrs. Benham had pasted red and yellow cardboard leaves on some of the kindergarten windowpanes. I could almost hide behind them as I peered inside.

I saw feet under the tables. Girls' sandals, boys' sneakers. Knobby knees with round brown scabs. Travis's knees. I ducked under a maple leaf so I could see his face. His blue eyes were swimming with tears and his cheeks were wet.

If only I could go inside! If only I could speak! I'd say, *Hold on, Travis. You can do this. Be brave.*

He looked up. I gave him a big wave and a huge smile.

He still cried.

I made a face, scrunching up my nose.

He wiped his cheeks.

I made a different face.

He began to smile.

There.

I ran inside again and stopped at the girls' room, a good reason for being out of the classroom.

When I opened Ms. Quirk's door, I could tell that no one even noticed I'd been gone.

No one but Mason.

He held up his partner note.

It said *Judith*.

And mine would say *Mason*.

CHAPTER 13

$\mathcal{I}$t was my afternoon with Mr. Kaufmann. I peered in the door window to see if anyone else was there. But he was alone, working at his computer, chewing at his bristly mustache.

This office was a great place. On the wall was a picture of a magician with a white rabbit, and on the table was a bowl of grapes. He'd told me he'd hung the picture when he first came to the school a hundred years ago.

I went inside. He looked up and held out his hands, front, and then back. I had to smile.

"Hello, Ms. Judith." He rolled his chair forward, lightly touching my ear. "What do you know? Here's a quarter." He held it up for me to see.

Sometimes it was a dime, sometimes a folded dollar. I never could figure out how he did it, but it made me laugh.

I liked the sound of my laugh, and he liked it too. "It's like a stream that bubbles up," he'd said once. "I think your voice will sound just like that. And I will hear it someday."

Maybe.

He'd known what I was thinking. "I am right. Magicians always are."

I was laughing again. I could almost picture a shiny top hat on top of his bushy hair. When I first met him, he'd told me he was the school psychologist, but he wasn't crazy about that title.

That reminded me of the doctor I'd seen a while back. He wore glasses that kept slipping down his nose as he played games with me, and was almost as much fun as Mr. Kaufmann. "You have selective mutism," he'd said. "You can certainly speak, but right now you're afraid to do that."

Selective mutism: a terrible title.

Today Mr. Kaufmann and I spent time leafing through my cartoon pad. It was his turn to laugh. He certainly didn't sound like a bubbling stream; it was more like a truck going uphill, sputtering all the way.

"So what's new?" he asked afterward.

I turned to a clean page. *I have a dog.*

He nodded. "That's the best."

I wrote again: *Someone said that nobody wants me.*

He didn't say anything for a moment. He shook his head. Then he turned the page over. "All right,

Ms. Judith. Make a list of everyone who does want you."

I began to write: Aunt Cora, of course, and Gideon. Dog. And Travis. Ah, and Ms. Quirk.

Could I add Mason's name? I wasn't sure. But why not?

"A decent list, to be sure," Mr. Kaufmann said.

Then he reminded me of our *take it easy* plan. Amazing—the name of Gideon's boat. But Mr. Kaufmann wouldn't know that.

He took a breath loud enough for me to hear; he raised his shoulders and lowered them a few times. "Ah, so relaxing." He popped a grape into his mouth and pushed the bowl toward me. "Every time I feel worried, that's what I do." He grinned. "Too bad I don't always have the grapes."

I could see it, a cartoon.

CHAPTER 14

*F*or the rest of the week, Ms. Quirk moved the class around. In math we even crawled on our hands and knees, measuring the classroom, the hall, and the front steps of the school.

Mason and I were partners. He did the ruler work; I did the writing down.

I began to notice things about him. No matter how neat he started out in the morning, he was a mess before the day was half over. He attracted dirt and spills like magnets attract metal.

I didn't mind. It wasn't important.

He was lucky. He lived in a house with a whole family: a mother, a father, a brother.

Another thing: he talked. Not just one word, not one sentence. He talked every other minute. And when he wasn't talking, he was whistling.

"Shhh." Sophie looked up from measuring with a yardstick. "I can't think straight, Mason."

I liked the sound of his talking, his whistling, his singing, the songs he made up. I looked in Sophie's direction, but she blew her bangs off her forehead.

I realized something. Mason and I were probably the most unpopular kids in the class.

I sat back on my ankles.

It was true. I was a weirdo who didn't talk. And he was Mason, a sloppy kid who talked too much.

But the weekend was coming up.

"Meet you tomorrow morning," Mason said when the dismissal bell rang on Friday. "Nine o'clock."

I remembered the shoe print at Ivy Cottage. Did he mean at the pond behind it? I nodded a little uncertainly.

The next morning, Dog and I turned up the road to Windy Hill when I heard a voice. "Where are you going, Judith?" Mason called from the path below.

Dog moved before I did. He bounded back to Mason, jumping and welcoming.

I walked toward them slowly.

"You're going the wrong way." Mason handed Dog a bacon strip.

What was he talking about? I followed him. He wasn't going anywhere near my pond.

We took the long walk along Shore Road, around

to the tip of the island. We stopped at a narrow strip of beach, empty and windswept.

I'd forgotten the old wooden pier that jutted out across the water. It was falling apart, with planks missing and pilings leaning against each other.

Mason didn't stop. He walked carefully, raising one foot at a time, holding the railing that looked as if it might give way any minute.

He didn't go far, though; only a few feet.

Dog was too smart to follow. He sat on the edge of the sand, whining.

Yes, it looked dangerous. Aunt Cora would be shaking her head, warning me.

Mason lay on his stomach, yelling, "Come on!"

He wasn't looking at freshwater turtles, not in that salty sea.

"Judith!" he called again.

There was no help for it. I put my foot on the first plank, and then the second. I went one step further, and crouched down to see what he was looking at.

Dog was barking, taking a few running steps along the sand.

"I was never going to tell anyone about this." His voice was loud above the sound of the water as it swirled underneath us. Dozens of creatures, one on top of another, grasped the pilings. They were the color of metal and looked like tanks.

A filmy jellyfish floated nearby.

And fish! Dozens of fish, a few small as my pinky nail, others fist-sized, swam around a wooden plank on the seafloor.

Mason pointed to a sea star.

He leaned on his elbows. His dark hair was damp and curled from the sea wind. "I'm not telling you because you can't tell anyone. It's because you're . . ." He hesitated. ". . . my partner."

Just for a second, I glanced at his gray-green eyes.

I looked down at that world of ocean creatures.

Mason hadn't meant to say *partner*. I was sure of it. He'd meant to say *friend*.

He must have known I'd never had a real friend.

And maybe he'd never had a real friend either.

For that moment, I didn't care about speaking, or that everyone thought I was a weirdo.

I was reminded of something Ms. Quirk had said a couple of times. *When you get to know something, you appreciate it. It's the same with people.*

Mason said, "It's a whole world down there. Why should we just write about turtles? Why not all of this?" He swept his arm around and I felt the plank beneath me tremble.

Why not?

We grinned at each other.

"And you"—he pointed—"can draw all of it."

I nodded.

"It will be spectacular." I almost laughed. Aunt

Cora liked to say spectacular too. We crept off the pier to the sand. Then Mason pulled out paper from his pocket and bent his head to write down some of what we'd seen.

Later, we walked back along the Shore Road, the sun warming our heads.

We saw Sophie on the way.

"I guess she didn't see us," Mason said as she passed, her face turned away.

Fall

CHAPTER 15

*O*n Monday at school, Harry howled so loud it made me jump. And Conor was laughing, almost like a donkey.

"Sounds like a hyena project for the two of them," Mason whispered under his breath. "Fits, doesn't it?"

But whoever heard of a hyena on our island?

Mason and I were keeping our project a secret. He bent over his paper, writing, scratching out, writing again, as I drew cartoons of sea robins, those fish with wings, chirping.

Mason wanted us to find a leatherback turtle. He kept talking about it.

"Listen, Jude . . ." That was what he called me now. "They're huge, the largest of all the sea turtles. Sometimes they're six feet long, and they can travel a thousand miles in a couple of months; one even traveled almost three thousand miles in four months."

I nodded a little, surprised that he knew so much.

He kept whispering. "They're amazing. I've seen pictures, dark gray to black, with white speckles. We need to keep our eyes open. They'll be on the lookout for jellyfish. They love jellyfish the way I like Oreos."

I gave a sideward glance at the remains of an Oreo on his shirt.

Cold-blooded. I wrote.

He glanced at my paper and hesitated. "Leatherbacks aren't as cold-blooded as freshwater turtles. Their temperature is a little higher than the water they swim in."

Interesting. More interesting was learning about Mason. With his ripped shirts and muddy jeans, somehow I didn't realize how much he knew.

But I knew what he was thinking now. Ms. Quirk had told us there'd be a prize for the most original project when we showed our projects to our parents in October.

"You can't get any more original than knowing about a leatherback that's traveled three thousand miles." He wiped fingers on his shirt. "And can you imagine seeing one?"

Wouldn't it be something: winning a prize!

And so after school, we wandered along the dock, circled the wharf, and took a few steps on the old pier, eyes down, searching the water.

But there was much more on my mind than leather-back turtles swimming near our island.

Suppose we compared them to freshwater turtles?

I'd have to give up a secret, though.

Mason would have to see the pond in back of my falling-down Ivy Cottage.

Why not? I kept asking myself. But it was hard to let go of that secret place.

Still, I'd do it.

Gideon came looking for me after school on Friday.

I'd just dropped my books on my bed and was at my window, toeing my feet into water-walking sneakers, when I saw him at the edge of the path and waved.

He looked up and put his finger on his lips, then motioned for me to come downstairs.

Aunt Cora's birthday was in two weeks. Gideon and I always had a three-person party for her. And now Dog would be there. Gideon must have been thinking of presents: he always had the best ideas. And this year I'd drawn a picture of Aunt Cora speeding along on a motorcycle.

Aunt Cora was whistling in the kitchen, pulling pots out of the cabinet, so it was easy: I tiptoed out the front door and closed it silently behind me.

"How about a walk, Red?" Gideon asked.

He didn't look exactly like himself. He tried to smile beneath his beard, but he looked . . . was it worried?

I raised my eyebrows in a question as we walked down toward the ferry slip.

"It's about you, my girl."

Me? Not the birthday?

"A long story," he went on. "Just between the two of us, now."

I nodded.

"When you came to live with Cora, she was happier than she'd ever been. She said you were a miracle. I was glad too, more than glad. We'd be a family."

He shook his head. "But Cora didn't think that was a good idea. She wanted to spend all her time taking care of you, loving you."

I squinted out toward the water, the sun high and warm, trying to remember those early days. I could see the hall and Aunt Cora's arms out.

"I want to ask Cora again," he said.

What was he talking about?

But then I heard footsteps. Was it Mason? Waiting for me to go turtle hunting with him?

I turned—yes, Mason. But he was tearing along Shore Road, his brother close behind, arms out. Trying to catch him?

Gideon was smiling at me, that uneasy smile again. "It would mean I'd be your almost-father. So I have to ask you first if that would be all right."

I'd never thought about a father. My own father wasn't real. Not only did he have a question mark face, I didn't even know his name.

But Gideon, an almost-father. He was talking about marrying Aunt Cora. Imagine. I began to smile. But Mason was running back along the road, his shoulders hunched, crying.

Mason crying?

I knew he wouldn't want me to see him that way, so I pretended I was looking up at the dirt road that led to Windy Hill.

Next to me, Gideon said, "Guess not, right, Red?"

I shook my head. I nodded. I smiled. I opened my mouth to say it was fine, it was wonderful.

But nothing came out.

And it was too late. Gideon patted my shoulder. "It's all right. It was just an idea."

He went away from me quickly, out onto the ramp, and disappeared onto the waiting ferry.

I would have gone after him, but the warning horn sounded; he'd be pulling away. And Aunt Cora would be wondering where I was. But I'd draw a cartoon for him. It would say I liked his idea. I loved his idea.

CHAPTER 16

Leaves drifted outside the window. It was Saturday: Aunt Cora's birthday.

Gideon came up the path with a chocolate cake from a bakery near the ferry stop on the mainland.

"Surprise!" he boomed as he opened the kitchen door.

I knew Aunt Cora really wasn't surprised. We did this every year. But she opened her eyes wide, and covered her mouth with her hand. "Oh, my. I can't believe it."

She opened the box he handed to her. I leaned forward to see. It was a necklace with a motorcycle dangling from the silver chain. She looked at me, smiled, then leaned over to hug Gideon. "I love it. It's the only speed you'll get from me!"

She loved the book a friend had sent too, and she always had tears in her eyes when she opened my present.

This year I'd found a jasmine plant covered with white blossoms on Windy Hill. I'd potted it up in a yellow planter from the shed, and covered the whole thing with Christmas paper turned inside out, and two of my gold hair ribbons.

"Oh, Jubilee," she said. "You are everything to me."

That made me think of Gideon wanting to be a family. I had to give him the cartoon I'd made.

I'd done something else. I'd sneaked Aunt Cora's birthday cards out of the mailbox during the week so she could open them all at once. One of them was from my mother. I'd seen that handwriting dozens of times.

Usually she read all of them aloud.

But not this time.

She read my mother's card, then tucked it under her plate and went on to show us the others.

After we ate, I went outside to give Dog a birthday treat, a double dog biscuit, thinking about that card.

It was still there when I came back, and Aunt Cora had gone to check on the altar flowers for tomorrow's Mass. And Gideon had gone to the ferry.

I took everything else off the table—crumpled napkins, glasses, the cake plates—until there was nothing left but Aunt Cora's plate with the envelope tucked underneath.

I couldn't leave them there.

I wiped my sticky hands on a birthday napkin. Why was I sure the card was from my mother? The return address was in the town where the ferry docked on the mainland.

Would Aunt Cora mind if I looked at it?

She never minded anything I did. *I love you, Jubilee. I've never loved anyone as much as you.*

I slid the plate out of the way and picked up the card.

That's what it was.

A birthday card from Amber. Amber, my mother.

Her handwriting was big and loopy and the *is* were dotted with circles:

Dear Cora,

You know I can't stay in one place very long. Now I've come back to Maine, to Smith Street. I have a job in a bookstore. I miss my girl. I wish things had been different. I don't know if you want to tell her that I'm here from California.

If you think it might upset her, then don't. I leave it up to you.

Love,
Amber

I sank onto the chair. I was the girl Amber missed. She was the mother who wished things had been different. That's what I wished.

I put the card back under the plate, even though

they looked strange on the bare table. But they were blurry now; my eyes were filled, my throat tight.

I went down the hall to my bedroom and opened the window wide so the sea air could blow over my face.

Then I lay down with Dog until Aunt Cora came home. I heard her begin dinner, the refrigerator door opening and closing, the pots rattling on the stove.

I knew she was putting my mother's card away somewhere. She must have been trying to decide what to do. And knowing Aunt Cora, it would take a long time. Too long.

How could I wait?

CHAPTER 17

*T*he next morning, Aunt Cora pointed at two woolly bear caterpillars that were wandering around. They were the color of chocolate candy; that meant a cold winter.

Good. I loved the snow on the island and the dark nights when I could read in my robe and my fuzzy slippers. Did my mother love snow? Did she know about woolly bears?

I wanted to know so many things about her. Suppose . . . I shook my head.

But Aunt Cora was leaning over the last of the tomatoes. This morning she'd cut them carefully. The kitchen would steam and the windows mist as they simmered.

"A jubilee of tomatoes!" She handed me a perfect red one, warm from the sun. "Just like your Pippi Longstocking hair."

It was a perfect fall day. I bit into the tomato's soft

skin. The sky was a sharp blue, and apples dotted the trees along the road.

I hugged her, then hurried to meet Mason at the wharf, dozens of cartoons in a folder under my arm.

I'd made up my mind. Mason was truly my friend. How could I not show him the pond? I wanted to show him the bale of turtles sunning themselves on that lacy log, or hiding deep under the clear water.

Mason waited down on the road. He wiped his jeans that had two dirt spots, round as the apples on the trees. "Hey, Jude!" he called.

I beckoned, pointing to the road that led up to Windy Hill.

"Wrong way."

I kept going, looking back over my shoulder.

He shrugged, then caught up to me.

Lemon-colored leaves shimmered on the trees as we climbed, and then Dog gave a little whine.

It was Travis, twirling beside a twisted little pine, using a small blue blanket for wings, or maybe a tent.

Sophie was nowhere in sight.

Travis stopped twirling and waved, then hid himself under the blanket. Mason and I grinned at each other and kept going until I saw the tangled mass of ivy that covered the walls of my cottage.

We walked around to the pond. I felt the excitement in my chest. I couldn't wait to see what he'd say. And then we were there.

He stopped. "Oh, Jude. Wow."

We smiled at each other and I pointed to the turtles on the bank, four or five of them, one almost on top of another, their heads raised to the sun, their legs splayed.

"We could write . . . ," Mason began.

I nodded, pulling him down to sit on a pair of rocks that edged the pond. I showed him my cartoons: turtles on a log, piled sky high; turtles snapping at frogs; turtles pulling in their heads as an egret went by. It was all there, everything I knew about them.

He was grinning. "You're the best."

We heard the blast of the ferry horn. "I'm supposed to be home," he said. "I have to go."

I waved. I wanted to stay. There was something I wanted to do. Dog and I waited, watching Mason run down the path.

I made my way to Ivy Cottage, pushing back the stone and ducking inside.

I was drawn to the silver mirror in the bedroom, the place where I could talk. I sank down in front of the mirror. "I want to see my mother."

What had her card said? *I miss my girl.*

"Then why did she leave? What was wrong with me?"

Dog came in and sat next to me. I stared at our reflection in the mirror. "I can't wait. I'm going to go to her."

I sat back. "Yes," I said. "Somehow. I'm going to see my mother."

Would I stay forever, or just a few days? Would she really want me there?

"Tomorrow night. That's when I'll leave." I took a loud breath, and raised my shoulders the way Mr. Kaufmann did. *Take it easy.*

"I can do this."

I left the bedroom, Dog following. I was a little afraid, but I knew my plan was right.

Dog and I went back along the road slowly, passing Travis halfway down. "I'm a giant!" he yelled, grinning at me. With a front tooth missing he looked more like a small jack-o'-lantern.

I grinned back at him. I made the scariest face I could think of, and curled my fingers into giant's claws.

He loved it.

But Sophie appeared out of nowhere. She must have seen my face, because she shook her head. Without saying a word, she took Travis's hand and led him away, walking around us, almost stepping on my foot.

I opened my mouth, but what could I say? No wonder she thought I was weird.

Never mind. I had a friend. I had a mother.

CHAPTER 18

$\mathcal{I}$ sat with my quilt wrapped around me and Dog lying across my feet, thinking of how it might be. I'd knock on my mother's door and wait until she answered. What would she say? Would she reach out and put her arms around me?

And how was I going to get there?

I closed my eyes. First, I'd need to get off the island without anyone seeing me. I wasn't invisible after all.

I remembered Mason hiding in that boat. Suppose I borrowed one? But I'd have to leave it on the other side. The owners would search and search, and maybe they'd never find it.

The word *stealing* came into my mind.

What about taking the ferry?

I'd hide in one of the ferry closets, leaning against the canvas hoses and extra life jackets, just in case someone I knew was on board.

Smith Street. I remembered that. But what was the number. Suppose there were a dozen houses? Two dozen?

I'd have to find that card again.

The next day was Monday; that night I'd leave. I ate my breakfast and went to school.

I kept glancing at the clock on the classroom wall for the rest of the long day. When the dismissal bell rang, I was the first one out the door. I had to be home before Aunt Cora. I was glad she walked slowly, that she took her time admiring the birds that fluttered from tree to tree, and the plants along the road.

I'd search. She squirreled things away in her sewing box, or in the kitchen drawers. You could find things just anywhere.

I found the sewing box, but the card wasn't under the messy spools of thread; it wasn't in the side pockets with the tiny glass buttons that belonged to one of my long-ago baby dresses.

I spent the next half hour searching the cabinets, the drawers with the knives and forks, the pantry closet.

It wasn't in the kitchen.

I glanced out the window. Aunt Cora wasn't coming up the road.

The card had to be in her bedroom.

How could I go in there? Aunt Cora never came

into my room without knocking. She never opened my dresser drawers to put things away without asking.

I shook my hands in front of me, ready to cry. Without that address, I wouldn't find my mother.

The living room clock chimed once: four-thirty. I rushed down the hall and into Aunt Cora's bedroom.

I touched the gold and green quilted bedspread and the top of her shiny dresser. I opened one drawer at a time, looking down at her boxes of earrings, her pajamas and rolled-up socks.

I knew it was wrong, even as I ran my hands underneath her sweaters, then opened the bottom drawer.

Inside were a few scarves, a pair of woolen gloves, papers in uneven piles. It would take forever to look at it all.

Aunt Cora might be walking toward the house right now.

I scrambled through the pile; I found birthday cards I had made for her, and a heart scribbled over with a red crayon for Valentine's Day when I was five.

Did I hear the front door open?

There was the envelope! In the corner it said *416 Smith Street.*

I'd find her.

She'd open the door. *I knew you'd come someday,* she'd say.

Aunt Cora called, "I'm home, honey."

I closed her drawer, smoothed the quilt, then darted into my room and sank down on the bed, out of breath.

I'd done something terrible. If I could talk, I'd have told Aunt Cora.

After a while, Gideon came for dinner, his big voice filling the room. "Monday night, meat loaf and mashed potatoes. What could be better?" He winked at me.

It was our least favorite meal, and Aunt Cora laughed.

I hardly ate, thinking ahead to tonight.

Back in my room, I wrote a note to Aunt Cora:

I love you, but I want to see my mother.

I've always wanted that.

But what would I do without Aunt Cora? What would she do without me?

CHAPTER 19

$\mathcal{I}$ tiptoed to the window without making a sound. It was late. The moon shone down on the garden; but the road was dark and still. I opened my bedroom door. The light in Aunt Cora's room was out.

I thought again about what I'd bring with me. I couldn't carry much, and there wouldn't be room in the hose closet on the ferry for much more than me.

I shrugged into my jacket and tucked my cartoon pad in my pocket. I had more than enough money to pay for the ferry.

I could take one thing to read, a paperback. I ran my finger along the row of books on the shelf and took the story of a pioneer girl.

I listened: Aunt Cora slept. I tiptoed down the hall and opened the front door without a sound. Dog padded along right behind me.

Dog!

How could I have forgotten!

I sank down next to him and felt the soft fur on his back, his velvet ears. I leaned close so he could give my face a quick kiss.

How could I leave him?

But I couldn't take him with me.

The ferry horn blasted; the last one would leave in thirty minutes.

Aunt Cora would take care of him, but it wouldn't be the same. Dog needed a kid who loved him, who would run with him and curl up with him at night. A kid who would love him the way I did!

I pictured a big house with a rickety fence all around it.

Mason's house.

Mason loved Dog. And Dog would love Mason.

They'd be happy together at the pond. They'd search the seawater for a leatherback turtle.

I dropped a kiss on top of Dog's head and put a note for Mason in Dog's collar. "I love you," I whispered. I made myself stand up.

I went back and added quickly to the note I'd written to Aunt Cora. I had to tell her where he was.

Dog followed me as I ran to Mason's house. I opened the gate and pointed, until Dog realized I wanted him to go into their yard.

And that's what he did. When I shut the gate, his head went down, his tail waved from left to right, an unhappy wave. He made a sound deep in his throat. I stood there for a moment, crying. Dog and I belonged together.

He cried too as I ran to the ferry, my hands over my ears.

If only Mason would hear him and come outside.

I bought my ferry ticket. Luckily, I didn't know the ticket person. I was the last one through the gate, hurrying up the gangplank and inside.

My hand up, half hiding my face, I went along the aisle so no one would recognize me, or wonder why a girl would be on the ferry by herself this late.

I tucked myself into the hose closet on the main deck as the ferry gave a warning blast and set off onto open water.

The air was close; it smelled like kerosene, or engine fuel. It was sickening. I tried to take small breaths as I scrunched up on top of a coil of heavy rope.

I closed my eyes, thinking of Dog and Mason together, and Aunt Cora, who wouldn't see my note until morning. Ms. Quirk. Gideon, who wanted to be my father and didn't know I wanted it too. I'd forgotten his cartoon. Sophie, who'd be glad I was gone.

I felt the warm tears on my cheeks.

I pictured my mother, who missed me, and who would hold out her arms.

It seemed forever until the ferry bumped to a stop.

I hurried off before the captain could see me. Outside, I took deep breaths of the cold sea air, and stood in the shadows of the parking lot. Car doors began to open and shut, one pulling out after another.

I waited, trying to get my bearings. And like magic, I saw the sign under the light: *Smith Street.*

It was a good omen.

I began to walk. I was tired and cold, but I was almost there.

I took a guess and went to my right, where houses were attached to each other, but it was hard to see the numbers in the darkness.

I walked for blocks before I realized I was farther away from where I should probably be, and turned back.

Only a few houses had lights, and even the streetlights overhead seemed dim. I shivered as I retraced my steps. I was alone in the street, alone in that strange place. How strange it felt without Dog at my side, without the familiar sounds of the island.

At the crossroads, I went the other way. I peered at the numbers: 420, 418, and there it was: 416. I looked up at the brick house that was almost the color of my hair. No lights glowed in any windows, upstairs or down.

I swallowed, and was suddenly uneasy about waking her. Should I curl up somewhere and wait until morning?

But then I saw a pinprick of light above the bell on the door.

I made myself go up the narrow front path and press that bell. I waited to hear footsteps, but it was quiet.

I put my hand against the wooden door, staring at the lion knocker. How could I rap that knocker and make a noise that would wake everyone in the houses around me?

What could I do?

I was ready to sink down, my head against the door, and close my eyes. Imagine if she found me there, sleeping, in the morning.

But then—footsteps.

Coming down the stairs?

Down the hall?

I squeezed my hands together to stop their shaking.

I'd pictured this so many times: my mother opening the door and seeing me.

This was the time I was going to speak.

The door opened and a woman peered out. Her hair was thick and red like mine, but much straighter. She was taller than Aunt Cora, younger, thinner. She hesitated, lips trembling.

I opened my mouth.

I tried to say *Judith.*

I tried to say *Mother,* but I didn't make a sound.

I didn't have to, though.

She opened the door wider, and put out her hands to touch my shoulders.

CHAPTER 20

$\mathcal{S}$he pulled me into the hall, hands still grasping my shoulders. We stared at each other in the dim light.

Her question-mark face was gone; it would never come back. Her real face was familiar, with blue-gray eyes like Aunt Cora's. Freckles like mine.

She snapped on lights as we went down the hall and into the kitchen. "I knew you were coming," she said. "Judith? Is that what they call you?"

I nodded. What would I call her?

She shook her head. "I'll have to get used to that. I've called you Jay all these years." She waved me into a chair. "Like a blue jay, the bird, you know?"

Jay. Not my name. Not my name at all.

It was almost as if we were strangers. We *were* strangers.

She brushed back her hair. "Cora called me a few minutes ago to tell me you were coming. She wanted me to watch out for you. She asked me to call when you arrived."

Her fingers went to her hair again. "I would have met you at the ferry, if I'd known sooner."

It didn't matter. I had done it. I was sitting in my mother's kitchen.

My mother, the stranger.

Aunt Cora had awakened; she knew I was gone. I felt a sharp pain in my chest. Did she think I didn't love her?

My mother—Amber, I'd call her in my mind—picked up the phone. I heard Aunt Cora's voice as Amber told her I was there.

She spoke for just a moment. "She looks fine, don't worry." When she put down the phone, she said, "Cora said to tell you it was all right, that she understands."

Why did I have this pain? It wasn't exactly all right; it didn't feel the way I'd imagined it. Strange.

She opened the refrigerator. "Not much in here. We'll shop tomorrow." She pulled out a container of orange juice and poured two glasses. "I'm a mess in the kitchen."

I watched her move around, wearing a purple bath-robe that was soft as fur, a button missing on top. She opened a box of cookies and slid them onto a plate.

"You'll have to stay alone for a while tomorrow. I have to work. But we'll settle you in and talk about all this in the morning."

I didn't try to answer. I knew words weren't coming. I took a sip of juice and a bite of a cookie. Suddenly I was tired. Bone-tired, Aunt Cora would have said. Bushed, Gideon would have said. And Dog would have yawned, his jaws opened wide.

I yawned now too, quickly covering my mouth.

"Of course," Amber said. "Upstairs. The extra bedroom is a little cluttered." She smiled. "Not a little, a lot. But we'll manage. Jay—Judith, we'll manage. Step by step, we'll get it together."

I finished the juice and she went up ahead of me to a room at the end of the hall. It was small. It might have been cozy, but I was too tired to think about it as she said good night.

She turned back from the door, and reached out. She ran her hand over my hair, which was so much like hers, and gave me a quick hug. I watched as she padded down the hall to her bedroom.

She hadn't told me why she'd left, what had been so wrong.

But maybe tomorrow.

I tossed my jacket over the end of the bed, toed out of my sneakers, and pulled the quilt up to burrow underneath it. I stretched out my feet, feeling something missing.

Dog wasn't curled up at the bottom of the bed, resting on my feet, keeping them warm.

Oh, Dog. Suppose he was still outside all this time,

with no one to be with him? If only Mason knew he was there. If only he'd taken him in. Dog would be on his bed now, warm and safe. But I couldn't be sure of it.

What about my mother? Amber, who looked like Aunt Cora, whose hair was almost like mine? How did I feel about her? I just didn't know.

I must have slept; I dreamed, but not of Aunt Cora or Gideon, not even of Mason and Dog. I dreamed of a bale of turtles playing and afterward sunning themselves on a lacy log.

Early in the morning, I slipped out of bed and knelt below the window. In the distance the water was gray with small whitecaps, and the ferry, like a toy, was halfway across.

The island rose up, almost hidden, but green and lovely. Not my island anymore. Suppose I never saw it again, or Aunt Cora and Gideon? Suppose I never saw Dog? I bit down hard on my lip.

I heard footsteps going down the stairs. Amber was awake. I found the bathroom and ran warm water over my face and brushed my teeth with my finger. And then I was ready to go downstairs . . .

To see my mother.

CHAPTER 21

On my way down the hall, I heard her humming. It was a good sound, happy. I took a breath and went into the kitchen.

She turned and smiled. "Good morning."

I froze.

"I know," she said. "Don't worry about talking. Cora told me . . ." Her voice trailed off. "Don't worry about anything. We'll work it all out."

I smiled then.

She poured orange juice again, and pushed the plate of cookies toward me. "We'll get cereal later, maybe eggs." She leaned forward. "You can stay as long as you want; I want you to know that." She held my wrist. "It's strange, isn't it, seeing each other?"

She knew how I felt, and she was feeling the same way.

But what I wanted to know most of all I couldn't ask. Why had she left me? What had I done?

I pursed my lips and blew just a bit of air through them, almost as if I wanted to whistle. But there was no sound, and she glanced at me quickly before she pulled out a chair and sat down.

She was crying. "I'd be furious if I had a mother who'd just walked out. I've been angry at myself for all these years."

I leaned forward. Maybe I'd hear it now. What I'd done. What was wrong with me.

But she glanced up at the clock. "I have to go to work at the bookstore. I'd ask for the day off, but I did that last week. And I'm late even now. Do you think you'll be all right? I'll be back as soon as I can."

I nodded.

Just before she left, she reached up to a shelf and picked up a shell. Long and narrow, it was a swirl of a shell, covered with small brown squares.

"It's a junonia. I found it on the island one day." She put it in my hand. "If you'd like it, it's yours. Keep it in your room."

I put my fingers over the smooth shell, remembering what Ms. Quirk had said. *Maybe someday I'll find one.*

Amber reached for a leather jacket and went out the back door. "You'll be all right, Jay? The store's number is on the refrigerator."

I waved. Then everything was quiet. At home I would have heard the foghorn, or the ferry nosing into the slip, maybe church bells.

After I washed and dried the glasses and wiped off the table, I went to investigate: a living room with a couch and two flowered chairs, a dining room with chairs marching around a dark wood table.

Upstairs, the bedroom doors were open.

I remembered going into Aunt Cora's bedroom. Now she knew I'd found the birthday card in her dresser drawer.

What did she think? That I didn't care about her, that I wasn't a jubilee after all? And how would she tell Gideon I was gone?

What would Mr. Kaufmann say to me?

I went into the bedroom. A few boxes were piled in the corner; a framed picture of a city street hung on the wall, a little crooked.

I dragged the boxes into the hall closet and closed the door on them. Then I scraped the bed across the floor so I could look out the window and see the wires that stretched across the back of the houses, and much further, the water, and the smudge of the island.

I pulled out my book to read about a pioneer girl named Laura, but the words ran into each other, and it was hard to pay attention.

I stretched and went back down to the kitchen. Maybe I could find something for lunch. Maybe I'd cook dinner. I'd watched Aunt Cora almost every night as she put potatoes on to bake and vegetables on to boil.

Nothing was in the kitchen cabinets except salt and pepper and a jar of apricot jelly. No wonder Amber was so skinny.

There was money in my jacket pocket. I stood at the window, watching the street, which was much busier than the ones on the island.

Ms. Quirk would say, *Go for it, Judith*.

And so I went out the front door, making sure it didn't lock behind me.

CHAPTER 22

At five o'clock, Amber stood in the kitchen doorway. "I smell bread toasting. I see eggs frying."

She swooped toward me, put her arms around my waist, and twirled me around the table. "You're a genius." She laughed as we danced around the kitchen.

She made me laugh too; she made me happy. I put my hands on her arms as we twirled, and as I did, I glanced toward the stove. The eggs were burning.

I pointed, but for another moment, she wouldn't let go.

Then we were apart, both a little out of breath, as I turned the eggs with a spatula. She sat at the table, waiting. "No one has done this for me in years," she said. "And I certainly couldn't do it for myself."

I put toast and butter on the table, and even the jar of apricot jelly.

"I'm in heaven," she said.

I dumped the eggs on two plates and sat too. I liked the way she ate, the bites she took of the toast, the look on her face. "You made such a great meal." She hesitated. "Could I ask you . . ."

I tilted my head.

"I've called you Jay for so long. It's because of a bird we saw together when I was still on the island."

Jubilee. Red. Judith. Jude. All good names. And now Jay. Why not?

I almost said it. I formed the words with my lips, but nothing happened. Instead, I nodded.

She hadn't seen my cartoons yet. So while we ate, I pulled out a pad and drew a stick figure holding a bird.

She closed her eyes. "I can't believe this. I can't believe you."

We finished the eggs and I brought out a little cake I'd made from a mix. It was high on one side, flat on the other. I'd tried to even it out with lots of chocolate icing that came from a can.

But it was terrible. I took a forkful, and made myself take another. Then I raised my hands over the cake, and made motions as if I'd toss it, but Amber kept eating, one small bite after another. "It's delicious," she said.

I shook my head. She didn't have to do that. But

she kept eating, until I pulled the plate away from her, grabbed my pad again, and wrote the words *EEEK. NOT BIRD FOOD.*

She was laughing again.

And so was I.

CHAPTER 23

The next three nights we went to a diner. It was warm inside, the windows steamy. "I wish I knew what you're doing all day," she said.

I smiled. Every day, I'd gone down to the water, a long way from the ferry slip. A cement path lined the edge for as far as I could see.

I'd walked along that path. The gray-green water was much deeper at the edge than it was at home. Still, I could see shells and fish that were larger than the little ones that darted near our wharf.

I'd found a tiny library, and in the afternoon, I'd tiptoed back to the children's section to leaf through books about turtles.

Now Amber leaned forward. "I wonder what you're thinking." Her voice was louder than usual, because a TV blared on the wall overhead, giving the weather.

A server came toward us. "I'm Ellie, and we have pasta tonight. It's really good."

Ellie had tried some, I could see that. Tomato sauce was smeared across the sleeve and the front of her shirt.

We both nodded.

Ellie's tomato stains reminded me of Mason. He would have loved wandering along the water with me. And Dog would have sat up on the rocks watching. I raised my hand to my chest, feeling that ache.

"I never stay in one place for long," Amber said.

What did that mean? What was she telling me?

Above us, on the television, was the weather forecast: heavy storms on their way.

"There are things I have to tell you," Amber said.

I sat up and nodded.

Amber tapped my wrist. "You want to know what happened to me."

I swallowed. Waited.

"I was seventeen when you were born. You were beautiful. Even then you had red in your hair."

Over our heads, the TV blared news about the storm. And the server stopped to talk when she brought our plates to the table.

But how could I eat?

Amber spread her hands wide. "I did everything wrong. If you cried, I didn't know how to comfort you. You began to walk, and then fell. Fell more than once. My fault." She raised her shoulders. "My own parents had died. Cora and I had only each other."

I could see it: Amber, who didn't know what to do.

"My friends were still in high school," she said. "And I was home with a baby doing everything wrong. All I could think of was escaping, going to California, becoming an actress, or at least something exciting, something new."

The TV: "A possible hurricane. Massive flooding over the weekend."

"And I knew that Cora would be a wonderful mother. All she'd ever wanted was a child to love. A little girl. You."

She shook her head. "I've always been sorry. But you deserved a better mother."

For the first time, I was almost glad I didn't speak. What could I say? How could I tell her how glad I was that she didn't think it was my fault?

We began to eat but put our forks down after a few mouthfuls. I could see she was worn out, and I was too.

But there was something she had to know. I took out my pad and drew a school. It took up most of the page. I drew children going inside.

"An apartment house?" she guessed.

I wrote *school* on top. Even I knew I couldn't wander around near the water all day. I had to go back to school.

I saw the shock on her face. "You see what a flake I am? You see? I never thought of school."

I couldn't help it. I began to laugh.

"What's today? Friday. Yes, Friday. The weekend's coming. And I have to work. But I'll be off on Monday and we'll start you off fresh and new."

We walked back to Smith Street and went up to our bedrooms early.

But I didn't sleep. What had Ms. Quirk said? Something like *You have to know a person to appreciate him.*

Did I know my mother? Not yet. Once, she was seventeen years old and didn't know how to take care of a baby, and then a little girl.

Amber, who didn't cook, who was always late for work, who didn't remember I needed to go to school.

I did love her. Didn't I?

I sat on the edge of the bed looking out. High over the streetlights, thick dark clouds moved fast across the sky. A few drops pelted the window.

I loved the rain on the island. If it rained on Saturday, Aunt Cora and I would put on our raincoats and dash out to the garden for supper vegetables.

It had been cozy in Mrs. Leahy's room, with the rain pattering against the window. Ms. Quirk's room would be different, maybe even better.

I pictured Saturday nights with Gideon. I saw his hands, his nails thick, showing me how to make rope knots on the boat, teaching me how to run the motor, telling jokes at the supper table that made Aunt Cora's eyes crinkle up.

Gideon, who didn't know how I felt about him.

Would he take Mason out on the boat in the rain?

But that was all right too. More than all right.

Something else. Something I'd done. It was on the edge of my mind. What was it? I knew it was important.

CHAPTER 24

*B*efore she left for work at the bookstore on Saturday, Amber pulled boots out of the jumble in the hall closet. "A pair for you, a pair for me." She waved her hand. "There's a raincoat in the closet upstairs."

She put her arms around me. "Be careful if you go out." We could hear the wind and rain getting stronger. "It's so lucky that you're on the mainland away from that windy island." She hugged me and went out the door.

Upstairs, I looked through closets filled with shirts and jeans, and pulled a raincoat off the hanger. The boots were too big; I put on an extra pair of socks, and my feet still needed to grow another inch or two.

Outside, rain spattered on the hood of my rubber raincoat and splashed up against my boots; puddles rushed along the curbs.

No one else was in sight.

I hurried toward the water, watching the ferry pull away in the distance, going home. "Goodbye," I whispered, even though I knew Saturday was Gideon's day off.

I wandered along the cement path, went closer to the edge, and crouched down to watch the water smash against the wall.

Seaweed waved underneath, and I could just see a school of fish and some jellyfish waving underneath. Even the sand on the bottom swirled up in angry whirlpools.

And then I saw it.

Imagined it?

But it was there, swimming along, slate-gray, speckled, the largest turtle I'd ever seen. Its head was stretched out, its neck wide, its clawed feet and legs moving forward deliberately.

Going south.

A leatherback turtle.

It didn't belong here. It had come from somewhere, on its way somewhere. Maybe it was going home, wherever that was. I watched it, my head close to the water, watched the turtle that almost belonged to Mason, and to me.

Then it was gone.

"Oh, Mason," I whispered.

He should have been with me to see it.

What was I doing here on the mainland instead of home?

On the island where I belonged.

I stood still, the rain pelting me. And then I realized what had bothered me last night. I'd done to Dog what Amber had done to me. I'd just left him. How had I done that?

Wrong. I put my fist to my mouth. I tried to see as the wind drove the rain across the water and great gray clouds turned the afternoon sky into night.

Still, I didn't have much time. The ferry would be back within the hour.

I raced across the parking lot, ran back to the house, and threw open the door. I should have left my boots in the hall, but instead I left wet spots on the stairs as I clumped up to my bedroom.

I tore a piece of paper out of my cartoon book and wrote *I love you, Amber. I've been happy to be with you.*

That was true.

Someday I'll come again. But it's time to go back to the island. My dog needs me. I know you won't mind if I take the raincoat and boots. I drew a heart underneath and signed it Jay.

I put the junonia shell and my cartoon book deep inside the raincoat pockets, but there was no time for anything else.

I took the stairs down two at a time, one hand sliding along the banister. I left the note on the hall table and went out the door.

The streetlights were on now, guiding me to the

ferry slip. As I ran, the warning sound of the horn blared.

Only one pickup truck and a van were in the parking lot. Who would be going to the island in this weather?

Only me. Going home.

The ticket taker's hair was soaked. "Crazy rain, right?"

I nodded.

"You live on the island, don't you? I think I've seen you. You're catching the last boat. We're shutting down."

So lucky that I'd made it!

I went downstairs to sit at one of the massive windows. I swiped at it, trying to see out. Where was the leatherback turtle now?

The ferry was like that turtle, lumbering along, steady even in this storm. I'd left everyone I loved: first, Aunt Cora and Gideon, and Dog. Especially Dog, who needed me.

My mother would be gone again someday. But I knew her now. I understood. But I'd never leave the people I loved again.

I remembered something Mr. Kaufmann once said to me: "You'll feel better when you understand yourself."

My face was reflected in the glass as the rain ran down the window. A wavery cartoon face.

I'd run to the house, to Aunt Cora, and put my arms around her wide waist.

Then, at Mason's house, I'd kneel on the muddy ground while Dog whined and kissed my face.

I took out my cartoon pad. I drew the leatherback carefully, showing the massive head and the short neck. I drew the tail, shorter than the legs.

On top, I wrote, *Heading for warmer waters, heading for home.*

I couldn't wait to show it to Mason.

CHAPTER 25

The trip seemed to take forever, but, at last, the wooden walls of the slip loomed closer, screeching as the ferry edged in against them.

Moments later, I slid down the ramp and ran along the muddy road, my huge boots holding me back. The wind blew the rain in my face and pushed against me, almost as if it didn't want me to reach home.

Arms out, I went up the back path and circled the flattened garden.

There were no lights on the porch. But I knew the electricity would be out. I opened the door, banging on the side of the wall so Aunt Cora would know I was home.

I could only hear the rain pounding on the roof. I went from room to room, up and down the stairs in the dark. She wasn't there.

I sank into a kitchen chair and pushed back my

hood. The ends of my hair dripped on my shoulders, the curls tight to my head.

Had she gone to the mainland? Would she have left the island?

Never.

Then it came to me. The church! That was where everyone would be. The generator would give them light and warmth.

I dried my hair with a kitchen towel. I'd never been so thirsty. How strange, with all the water I'd just come through.

I smiled, thinking of Gideon reciting an old poem in his deep voice: *"Water, water, everywhere, nor any drop to drink."*

I peered into the dark refrigerator. A glass bowl filled with syrupy fruit was on the top shelf. I pulled it out and held it to my mouth, gulping down the juice.

I pulled a spoon out of the silverware drawer, not even having to look. How well I knew this kitchen.

Home.

Dog and I would be together soon. If only he was all right!

I ate the pale grapes, the purple berries, and the orange slices, feeling them slide down my dry throat.

The wind moaned. It was almost as if I heard someone wailing with it. But I couldn't wait to go to the church.

As I went outside, the wind pulled the door out of

my hands and slammed it against the wall. I wrestled with it, closed it, and tried to run up the road.

Like the kitchen door, I was captured by that howling wind; I zigzagged across the road.

At the church, a dim light beamed through the red and blue stained glass windows. The doors were closed and heavy, almost too strong for me, but someone opened them for me and I slid into the vestibule.

Sophie held the door.

I looked over her shoulder, searching for Aunt Cora, Gideon, Mason.

And where was Dog? Was he lost outside?

The pews were filled and people stood in the aisles, singing a hymn Aunt Cora loved, about angels. Bowls of rust-colored leaves filled the altar: Aunt Cora's favorites.

Sophie's cheeks were chapped; her eyes were filled with tears. "Travis is gone," she said. "My father's out there, and my cousins. They're searching along the water, the wharf, the ferry slip. My mother is still at the hospital on the mainland. She couldn't leave her patients."

She raised her shoulders. "I tried looking, but he always hides from me." Her finger pointed at my chest. "He loves you better than me. . . ."

I shook my head, shocked.

"He said he wished you were his sister, never yelling at him."

No-Talk Girl.

Right now, I wished I could call him, yell for him like a true sister.

I turned. From the vestibule window, I saw the beginning of the path that wound up Windy Hill. I imagined tree branches cracking and splitting.

I'd never been so afraid. But I ran out the door into the driving rain. I knew my way; I could picture every rock, every tree, every turning.

A No-Talk Girl who'd wandered all over the island by herself.

Fallen power lines and trees crisscrossed the road. Rivers of muddy water ran down the hill.

Travis wasn't on the path. His hiding place under the trees was filled with water.

Why had I been so sure I'd find him?

Then I remembered the sandy shoe print in Ivy Cottage. Travis's print?

I went up the hill, bent over, holding on to whatever I could grab, a rock, a branch, until I reached the cottage.

I ducked through the door, trying to catch my breath. The rain drummed against what was left of the roof and ran down the walls. One end of the hall was a waterfall; the floor was covered with a slime of mud.

But then I heard . . .

over the howl of the storm . . .

a whine.

Not Travis.

A dog.

I slid along the caved-in hallway, arms stretched against the walls for balance, my heart beating somewhere in my throat.

Please let it be Dog.

And yes! He was curled up in the corner. His head came up, his flag of a tail thumped the slightest bit, and there was welcome in his great dark eyes.

He didn't come bounding toward me as he usually did.

Because wrapped around his neck was a small hand, fingers splayed out.

Travis lay behind him, asleep.

Oh, Dog. I'd never leave him again.

I curled up with them for a moment, my arms around them. Dog ran his rough tongue over the side of my arm, and Travis moved a little to get closer to me.

How had Dog found him?

Why wasn't Dog with Mason?

No matter. They were here with me.

Safe!

Sitting there with the wind howling, and the ferocious rain over my head, I'd never been happier.

I leaned against Dog's silky fur, his back warm, his thick tail still thumping.

By now Amber would know that I'd gone back

to the island. I hoped she'd understand; I hoped she would.

My eyes were heavy. I closed them, just for a moment, remembering the old song Aunt Cora used to sing to me at bedtime. Something about a sandman.

I sat up. This was no time to sleep.

CHAPTER 26

𝒥 had to bring Travis back to Sophie.

I rubbed his arms and pushed the hair off his face. He whispered, "Sophie," then opened his eyes. "No-Talk Girl."

I smiled and pulled him to his feet.

How could he go out there in jeans and a sweatshirt that didn't even cover his wrists?

I pulled off my raincoat, shook it out, wrapped it around him, and closed the Velcro strips.

The hood half covered his face.

"Superman!" He raised his arms, the sleeves dangling, and I hugged him to me, listening to the wind and the rumble of thunder underneath its howl.

But I couldn't be afraid. Sophie was waiting. Her family was searching for him.

I took Travis's small hand. Dog shook himself,

sighing. He was at my side as I made my way down the slippery hall.

I held Travis tighter and went outside. His eyes were almost hidden under the hood, but he was smiling.

"An adventure." He grinned, showing the space where his new tooth would come in.

More than an adventure. It was a miracle he and Dog had somehow reached the safety of Ivy Cottage.

On the way back, a small tree crashed in front of us, bouncing up, leaves quivering. Rivulets of muddy water filled with small branches and leaves coursed down the side of the road.

I planted my feet carefully in my boots, watching each step so I wouldn't fall or lose Travis's small hand.

Heads down, we trudged toward the lights of the church. We climbed the three steps and managed to push open the massive doors.

Sophie shouted, "Travis!" She wrapped her arms around him in that wet raincoat. Then she looked at me.

As he shrugged out of the coat, Sophie said, "Thank you forever, Judith." She was crying so hard I almost didn't hear what she said. "I hated that he loved you best."

I touched her arm. I shook my head. I wished I could say *You're his sister. How lucky you are!* But maybe she'd know it now. He hugged her as if he'd never let go.

Out on the steps, Dog hesitated. Maybe he knew he wasn't allowed in church. But I'd rather stay on the steps myself than leave him. I gave his collar a gentle tug, and he bounded inside.

A woman in the last pew turned. Her mouth opened: A dog in church? A girl dripping on the floor?

There! I caught a glimpse of Aunt Cora and Gideon.

Aunt Cora's hands went to her face.

People were crowded in the aisle between us. But they managed to move around everyone.

Then they were holding me, the three of us together, rocking in back of the church.

Dog wanted to be part of us; he nosed in around our legs, while people sang another hymn, "Amazing Grace."

Amazing . . .

Because Sophie's father had come into the church now, and I heard him crying as he called, "Travis!"

Mason somehow ducked between arms and bodies, until he stood in front of us, a mess as always. "Dog," he whispered. "Where have you been?"

He looked at me. "And you too, Jude. Where have you been, anyway?"

Maybe I'd be able to tell him someday. But for now

it was enough to grin and raise my wet shoulders in the air.

We stayed in the church for the rest of the night. A few people went downstairs to stretch out in the activities room. Others leaned against each other in the pews, trying to sleep. We sat with them, Dog at my side. Aunt Cora and I held hands.

The next morning, a pale light beamed through the stained glass. I raised my head over Aunt Cora's shoulder.

Something had changed.

The rain was slowing, barely making a sound against the roof.

Aunt Cora stirred. And Gideon whispered, but his voice was deep. "Rejoice."

People moved, gathering up packages, purses, and themselves. Someone opened the door, and one by one, they began to leave.

We walked home together, our boots covered in thick mud. Dog's fur was matted the way it had been the day I'd found him.

"Devastating," Aunt Cora said, stepping over a piece of tile from someone's roof.

"But we're here," Gideon said. "We've come through it."

Behind us, feet sloshed through the massive puddles. Mason called, "See you later, Jude. See you, Dog."

Dog turned and looked at Mason. I turned too. I knew Dog would stay with me. But he loved Mason too. If only I could say that to Mason. If only I could say *Thank you forever,* the way Sophie had.

Tucked into the pocket of the raincoat was my small cartoon pad. I couldn't wait to show Mason that leatherback heading south, heading home.

CHAPTER 27

"School will be closed tomorrow," Aunt Cora said.

I yawned, still so tired, but a little disappointed, because the junonia was in my raincoat pocket, a gift for Ms. Quirk. I was sure Amber wouldn't mind.

Poor Ciro, the janitor, would have to wash and scrub after the storm, dragging his pail behind him.

Gideon left to run the ferry across to the mainland. "I have miles to go before I sleep," he called back, words from a poem he loved.

But Aunt Cora and I went to sleep, and Dog slept at my feet.

How strange to be under the covers in the daytime!

I awoke starving. Aunt Cora broke eggs into a bowl to scramble and put bacon on to fry.

She shook her head. "All the herbs are ruined. No chives for our eggs, no basil. But I'm not complaining. It's a jubilee to have you home."

I ate the soft eggs, drank the apple juice and even a half cup of coffee laced with milk while Aunt Cora talked. "I couldn't come to you. I had to give you time with your mother. I'm glad she's home. I'm glad you were with her."

I pulled out my pad, but there was too much to say.

"I know," Aunt Cora said. "But now that she's just a ferry trip away, we'll make sure you see each other."

I pushed my chair back and went around to her, resting my head on hers. I didn't have to say anything. She knew it all.

But I had things to do. I tapped the molding to say I was going out.

Dog looked up at me and shut his eyes slowly. *Nap time.* He was worn out.

I patted his head, then went outside. Aunt Cora called after me: "Be careful."

Mason was at the wharf, watching the ferry lumber toward the mainland. He hadn't changed his shirt; it still had smears of mud.

"About time." He looked over his shoulder, grinning. "We have only a week to get our project ready."

He sounded as if I'd been gone a day at the most. He looked away. "How's Dog?"

I searched for an empty page in my cartoon book. *Dear Mason,* I wrote. *I'm so glad you kept him for me. I know you miss him. I wish . . .*

"It's all right." He put his hand over my pen. "Really. I knew you'd come back."

I flipped through the pad to find the cartoon to show him and held it out.

He stared down at it. "A leatherback. Really? Did you see . . ."

I nodded.

"If only I'd been there." He broke off. "I'm glad it was you."

He studied the drawing. "It's better than anything we could write," he said, leaving a muddy fingerprint at the bottom of the page.

But that was all right. That was Mason!

And he was going on about the leatherback that had traveled so many miles in a few months. "Someday I'll do that," he said. "My brother and I. We've planned a big trip."

I must have looked startled.

"We're friends sometimes."

We walked to the library together and were surprised to see it open. Newspapers were spread out on the damp floor. We were the only ones there, except for the librarian, who was running around mopping windowsills and clucking over ruined books.

We sat at a table, books on turtles and sea creatures piled high. Harry came in, racing for a back table, books on animals in his arms. Conor was right behind him. "We're going to win the prize."

For the next hour or so, Mason and I scribbled notes about crabs that clattered over the stones near the old pier, and jellyfish that did a slow ballet around them.

I heard the ferry horn; the boat was on its way back to the island. I touched Mason's arm, pointing toward the window, and the water.

"We've done enough for now anyway." He gathered up our books and papers.

Outside, I ran down the muddy path. The sun shone on the water, and diamonds sparkled in the gentle waves.

I waited, and waved at Sophie and Travis. People began to come off the ferry. Their mother hurried toward them and hugged them.

I climbed the ramp. Luckily, the ticket taker was nowhere in sight. I threaded my way around tables and chairs until I saw Gideon standing on the deck.

He turned, surprised. But only for a moment. I stood in front of him, my arms out.

My word was soft, but he heard it.

"Yes," I said.

His arms went around me. "Oh, Red. Oh, Jubilee."

And I said it again: "Yes."

CHAPTER 28

Thursday. Tonight was the night! Mrs. Ames and the parents were coming to school to see our projects. Ms. Quirk had scurried around with our class, setting everything out in the auditorium.

The junonia shell was on a small table in front. "The gift of a lifetime," she'd told me.

Now, at home, we scurried too. I slipped into a new green dress, the color of my eyes and the sea on a warm day.

Aunt Cora came out of her bedroom wearing her best blue dress and bent to push on heels. "They hurt." She winked at me. "My feet must be growing. But this is a special night."

Gideon smiled when he saw me. "That green is a redhead's color, for sure," he said.

We hurried to school. Who was going to win?

Harry and Conor with their island animals? Or maybe Sophie and Jenna, who'd written about squirrels?

It might even be Ashton and Maddie, with weird long-legged insects.

But Mason and I had a chance. My cartoons were pasted up on the wall with explanations underneath, the only project with drawings.

Maybe no one would notice a few misspellings, or a little mud, especially on the cartoon of the horseshoe crab. That one said *I look tough, but I'm a gentle guy.*

"This is wonderful." One father pointed to it.

"Fun!" That was Sophie's mom.

Mason's brother, Jerry, clapped him on the shoulder. "Not bad! Who would have thought?"

Mrs. Ames clumped up to the stage and praised all of us.

"Your teacher breathed new life into our school!" She smiled at Ms. Quirk. "And now, the winners!"

Mason and I couldn't look at each other. *Pick us, please!*

But we weren't the ones.

Harry and Conor gave each other a high five as they went up the steps to receive their medals.

Mrs. Ames held up her hand. "There's something else I want to say." She walked over to our project, taped up to the wall.

Oh no! The misspellings! The muddy fingerprints! My crazy cartoons.

She tapped one of my first cartoons: turtles sunning themselves on a log. She held it up. And then the leatherback.

She picked up Mason's papers. " 'Like our ferry, slow and heavy, the leatherback moves through the water,' " she read. " 'Schools of fish dart around the island. All on journeys.' "

Mrs. Ames said, "Judith and Mason, you did such a lovely job."

I caught Mr. Kaufmann's eye. He was smiling, nodding at us.

Mason and I glanced at each other as parents clapped. Did Mason feel the syrup in his chest the way I did? I nudged him, then held out a cartoon I'd folded into my pocket.

I'd drawn him in a messy shirt and uncombed hair. A ferry was coming toward him with a small golden retriever puppy on the deck. *We belong together, Mason,* said the blurb over the dog's head.

"Great-looking dog," Mason said.

Aunt Cora and Gideon came up to us. "A wonderful job," they were saying.

Gideon cleared his throat. "I'm bringing a dog from the mainland tomorrow. A surprise for you, Mason. Your mother knows. So does your brother."

And Aunt Cora said, "It's what Jude wanted. She's drawn a dozen pictures."

Mason and I grinned at each other. For a moment, he didn't say anything. Then he smiled. "You're a good friend, Jude."

After cookies and juice in the cafeteria, it was late when I went to bed, but I wasn't tired after such a wonderful night. I smiled at my saying "Yes" to Gideon.

Maybe I'd talk more now, because I hadn't done anything wrong. Not to Amber, or Sophie. Nothing had been my fault.

I was sorry Amber couldn't come to be with us. But she'd be here Saturday and Sunday. She'd stay with us and we'd tell her all about it.

And so much had happened. Mr. Kaufmann might say, "You made it happen, Judith."

I hoped so.

I fell asleep at last, thinking I'd draw all this for him.

CHAPTER 29

*T*wo days later, I spun around in front of the mirror. My flowered skirt went to the floor. I loved the silky white top.

The night before, at dinner, Gideon kept singing. "A happy day tomorrow." He winked at me. "It's my wedding day, a lucky day for Cora."

That Gideon! He always made us laugh.

It was almost time. Everyone would be there: neighbors, people from church, Gideon's friends from the ferry, half my class, and Amber. She might be late, but we wouldn't mind.

I went into Aunt Cora's room and put my arms around her. I breathed in her perfume and the sweet smell of her bouquet of roses on the dresser.

"Today," I whispered. "A jubilee."

ACKNOWLEDGMENTS

My students have made such a difference in my life, and in my writing. As I wrote this story, I thought especially of Christopher, Donald, and Anna. I pictured Scott Liam at my door. After all these years, I still look for Michael Gaffney.

How important my first class was! I remember all those long-ago students, and especially the four who made me love teaching: Sheldon Dreyfuss, Frank Noviello, John Sangimino, and John Wekerle. Shelly still keeps me smiling.

I treasure the memory of Ughondi Freeman Grant every day, my dear laughing girl.

Dr. Irving Rockoff gave hope and magic to our students; our friendship was warm and wonderful.

I'm more than grateful to Wendy Lamb, my editor and friend, who works tirelessly on my books. I thank her assistant editor, Dana Carey, for all she does; she and I have a shared love of dogs. Kathy Dunn is always there for me!

My family makes life worthwhile . . . especially Jim, who is everything to me.

ABOUT THE AUTHOR

Patricia Reilly Giff is the author of many beloved books for children, including the Kids of the Polk Street School books, the Friends and Amigos books, and the Polka Dot Private Eye books. Several of her novels for older readers have been chosen as ALA-ALSC Notable Children's Books and ALA-YALSA Best Books for Young Adults. They include *The Gift of the Pirate Queen; All the Way Home; Water Street; Nory Ryan's Song,* a Society of Children's Book Writers and Illustrators Golden Kite Honor Book for Fiction; and the Newbery Honor Books *Lily's Crossing* and *Pictures of Hollis Woods. Lily's Crossing* was also chosen as a *Boston Globe–Horn Book* Honor Book. Her most recent books are *Until I Find Julian, Winter Sky, Gingersnap, R My Name Is Rachel, Storyteller, Wild Girl,* and *Eleven,* as well as the Zigzag Kids series. She lives in Connecticut.

Patricia Reilly Giff is available for select speaking engagements. To inquire about a possible appearance, please contact the Penguin Random House Speakers Bureau at speakers@penguinrandomhouse.com.